TRACK ONE

Yay! Life is great in every way
I'm young and I care and I got so much to say.

Like the bee in the hive
I love being alive
Like a bird on the wing
I love to sing
Like a cloud in the sky
I love floating by.

Yay! Life is great in every way
Cos I'm young and I care and I got so much to say.

Like a fish in the flow – or a penguin in the snow
Or a monkey up a tree – or a dolphin in the sea
Or a crab on the sand – or a horse on the land

I'm young and I'm free and I'm gonna make a stand!

Sassy Wilde, age 13

PUFFIN BOOKS

Seriously Sassy *
Crazy Days

Hi! Have you ever felt like you do things for all the RIGHT reasons, then everything SPIRALS out of control in ways you could NEVER have imagined – and you're left wondering, how on earth did all that happen?

Well, that's why this book's called CRAZY DAYS. My life has been a total ROLLER-COASTER recently – some things have been BRILLIANT and others have been nothing short of DISASTROUS.

But, hey – I guess that's what being thirteen's all about . . . And that's why we all need fab BEZZIES like Taslima (cool and calm) and Cordelia (scary and stunning).

And at least I can hold my head high and say I TRY to do the right thing. Even when it all gets REALLY, REALLY tricky.

Oh, and I do my best to be a GOOD ROLE MODEL for my little sis, Pip (nine going on nineteen) – even though I suspect she's already got the world sussed better than I ever will.

One last thing – the whole BOY thing has got me BAFFLED! I mean, I thought it would be simple. You meet the Love of your Life, then it's pink clouds and sparkles all the way. Turns out it doesn't work that way. Sigh. Want to know more? Then read on . . .

Loadsalove,
Sassy :o) xxx

Books by Maggi Gibson

Seriously Sassy
Seriously Sassy: Pinch Me, I'm Dreaming
Seriously Sassy: Crazy Days

Everybody loves Sassy!

'I absolutely love your book, *Seriously Sassy*.
It's like you wrote it all about me!'
– Saskia, 10

'Your books are brill, Maggi! I've read *Seriously
Sassy* 17 times 'cause it was soo good! Can't wait
till the next one!' – Heather, 12

'I've just finished reading *Pinch Me, I'm Dreaming*
and I love this book! I'm rating it an "A"!' –
Guneet, 11

'You are my favourite author ever. I got your
book *Seriously Sassy* and didn't want it to end!' –
Mairi, 12

I

It's half seven in the morning and I'm in my Greenpeace nightie, playing air guitar and belting out, 'Yay! Life is great in every way!' when I stop in my tracks cos the tiger on my wall poster's staring at me accusingly with two sad amber eyes.

'OK, OK, Mr Tiger, I apologize! Life isn't quite as perfect as I make out in my song, what with all the forests getting chopped down and the rubbish piling up. But once I'm a famous rock-chica-extraordinaire I promise-promise-promise I'll fight global warming . . . and cruelty to animals . . . and pollution and everything else that our stupid parentals have done to mess up the planet.'

And with that I grab my robe and dash to the bathroom.

As I leap into the shower I run through the events of the last week that have made my life SO GOOD:

1. Y-Generation Music are almost 100% definitely gonna offer me a record deal – whoop whoop! . . . shampoo hair . . .
2. It's official! I have a boyfriend, the one and only Twig . . . rinse hair . . . AND I'VE HAD MY FIRST EVER KISS! Phew! At last. I'm thirteen and a half! . . . slap on Tame the Wild Beast conditioner . . .
3. I have the two bestest bezzies in the whole wide world – Cordelia and Taslima
4. Oh, and guess what? My long-running feud with Megan Campbell is over! We are now real buds again, if not quite best buds just yet.

I'm so happy I grab the showerhead like it's a mike and belt out again, 'Yay! Life is great in every way!'

The bathroom's totally steamed up now. It looks like that dry ice stuff you get on TV shows. As it swirls around me I imagine I'm singing my hit single to an audience of millions. (Ooops, totally naked – I don't think so!) 'YAY! LIFE IS –'

My prize-winning performance is rudely interrupted by a hysterical hammering on the bathroom door. 'SASSY!' screams my little sis. 'You've been in there for YEARS! Get out NOW!'

'Just coming!' I yell.

Quickly I rinse the conditioner from my hair and as I emerge from the shower cubicle I bow to my imaginary fans. Then I wind myself into a big fluffy towel and wrap a smaller one, turban-style, around my head.

'SASSY!' Pip batters her fists on the door again. (She's nine and two-eighths, but in my head she'll be forever two and two-quarters. Even when she's ancient, like twenty-five or something, I'll always see her as a pretty little toddler with a chocolate-smeared face.)

'SASSEEEE!!! I NEED TO GET IN NOW!' Pip shrieks so loud I swear my ears pop.

I finish brushing my teeth, wipe the steam from the mirror, flash myself a film-star smile, then throw the door open with a theatrical flourish.

'At last!' Pip gasps as she rockets past.

Discreetly I close the bathroom door. Some things are not meant to be shared. Even by sisters.

Twenty minutes later I've dried my hair, which, I regret to report, is more unruly than a roomful of toddlers on E-numbers, and I'm just pulling my despicable school polo shirt over my head when my mobile pings.

I dive on it – and can you believe it? It's a text from Magnus Menzies. At eight in the morning! That boy is NOT normal. I go to press Delete . . . but sad, sad, sad . . . I'm too curious! I don't actually WANT a text message from Magnus Menzies – we have BAD HISTORY – but isn't it weird that even when a text is from someone you don't want to hear from, it's almost impossible not to look at it!

While my mind's considering the weirdness of the human brain, my eyes read.

Hey Babes saw u on tv. WOW! C U @ skule.
MAGNUS xxx

XXX?!! From Magnus!!! Blaaargh . . . I'll need to brush my teeth again and gargle with some extra-zingy-minty-antiseptic mouthwash.

Five minutes later I swan into the kitchen. 'No, no, Miss Wilde isn't doing autographs,' I say, flapping a languid hand. 'Not before brekkie.'

'I was only wanting to say good morning,' Dad mutters as he puts the kettle on. 'And find out if Miss Wilde would like pancakes?'

Mmmmm . . . I had planned a zingy wake-me-up smoothie, but let's face it, I'm pretty woken up already – any more awake and you'd have to scrape me off the ceiling! Dad pours some batter into the hot frying pan. It sizzles enticingly and whispers, *Eat me, eat me, eat me.*

Mum yawns and looks over her spectacles. 'Your father's trying to get back into Pip's good books after last weekend's hamster fiasco.'

Dad looks glum. (Let's just say he was left in charge of Pip's hamster and, well, things didn't go according to plan. Which is somewhat worrying. I

6

mean, my dad's an MP. He's supposed to be running the country. But leave him alone with just one little hamster to look after – and we come back to chaos.)

Five minutes later me and Pip are scoffing Dad's delicious pancakes slathered in maple syrup. Pip has granted Dad Total and Absolute Forgiveness. Mum's quietly reading her book and Dad's hiding behind the morning paper. To the inexperienced eye we might even look like a normal family.

'Sassy,' Mum puts her book down suddenly. 'I'm worried.'

'I'm not surprised.' I lick some stray syrup from my fingers. 'The bee population's dying out . . . *lick lick* . . . and Einstein – you know that genius scientist dude . . . *lick lick* . . . – well, he said that if all the bees die out, then four years later the whole of civilization will collapse . . . *lick lick* . . . Something to do with food chains and things.' I gobble another piece of pancake. 'I'm pretty worried myself. The whole world's in meltdown. And what's worse – no one seems to be doing anything about it!'

'It's not civilization I'm worried about,' Mum sighs. 'It's you getting involved in this music business. I've just been reading about Arizona Kelly.'

I squint at the cover of her book – *Arizona Kelly: The Tragedy of my Success*.

'Mum!' I squeak. 'I hope you're not comparing me to Arizona Kelly! She's a complete bubble-head. She dropped out of school when she was twelve. She completely went for the fame thing. *And* she'll do anything to get on the front page of the papers!'

'It's true.' Dad taps his paper. 'She's on the front page again. Just got married –'

'So?' Pip protests as she lathers another pancake with maple syrup. 'Lots of people get married. *I* want to get married!'

'Well, I don't,' I say firmly.

'But Arizona Kelly's only sixteen,' says Mum.

'And it's her third marriage!' Dad adds.

'Hmmmpphhh . . .' Pip says with a waggle of her nine-year-old glittery pink fingernails. 'Sixteen's ancient.'

'Anyway, you don't need to worry about me turning out like Arizona Kelly,' I assure Mum. 'I want to be the best singer ever and write the best songs ever. Then I'm gonna use my fame and money to make the world a better place. I don't want to be an empty-headed star. Or a drug addict. Or married. OK?'

'Well, that's a relief, Sassy, but you really need to stick at your schoolwork too.' Dad folds his paper and takes off his frilly apron. 'You're too young to be sure about what you want to do with your life. So even if Y-Generation get in touch and offer you a record deal, and even if we do all agree that it's acceptable, you still need to get qualifications. Keep your options open.'

'Dad, I have only *ever* wanted to be a singer,' I protest. 'It's been my big dream for as long as I can remember –'

'Actually, that's not true,' Mum interrupts. 'When you were five you wanted to be a starfish.'

'Yeah, until I realized I had the wrong number of legs. Oh, and my head in the wrong place . . . Anyway,' I continue, 'I'm more mature now. I like my life the way it is. I don't want to change *anything*.'

'So if Y-Generation gets in touch while you're at school to offer you a recording deal, we'll tell them you're not interested?' Mum teases.

'No, Mum!' I squeal. 'You'll tell them I'm ready. Any time. Got that?'

'Course I've got it,' Mum beams.

'And I hope they do call, sweetie,' Dad says, ruffling my hair. 'You've worked hard to get this far. You deserve your big break.'

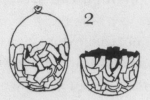

2

I'm not even inside the school grounds when Magnus Menzies homes in on me. Honestly! Can't he pick up the death rays I'm sending out?

'Hi, Sassy!' he grins. 'You look great!'

I give him a polite *thanks-for-the-compliment-now-go-live-on-another-planet* smile[1]. But Magnus does not understand the most basic body language. He just witters on about how wonderful I am. Which would be great if it was coming from the gorgeous Twig, say . . . or scrumptious Phoenix Macleod . . . But *Magnus*?!

A couple of tiny S1 girls with kohl-rimmed eyes that make them look like ring-tailed lemurs gaze on enviously. Unlike me they have still to learn that Magnus may look as tasty as an ice-cream sundae with a cherry on top, he may have gorgeous blue

---

[1] Cordelia taught me how. All teeth. No eye involvement. Hold for half a second max. Use sparingly and only on boys who deserve it!

eyes you could dive into, he may be a champion swimmer, *and* be pretty good at maths and science, but tragically he has the emotional intelligence of a mentally impaired mollusc.

'I thought you might like to do something after school? There's no swim practice today . . .' Magnus flashes me his perfect white-toothed smile.

I respond with a Force 12 withering look[2] – and what does he do? Only grins back at me with lovesick eyes!

Just then Cordelia comes drifting into the playground, clocks my predicament, and like a firefighter spotting a blaze, comes rushing to the rescue.

'Sorry, Magnus,' Cordelia says, her green eyes flashing as she links arms and leads me away. 'Sassy's not signing autographs right now. Come back in say . . . mmm . . . a hundred years?'

And with that we go giggling off towards the main entrance.

On the way to registration tons of people I don't even know high-five me and ask when my first single's coming out.

'I don't know yet,' I explain. 'But the recording company are getting in touch this week.' I'm amazed at how many saw the little clip of me on TV on Saturday night!

[2] Hurricane Plus

'You were only on for a couple of minutes,' Sindi-Sue gabbles while Miss Peabody marks the register. 'I was round at my big cousin's, vegging out on the sofa. The news had been droning on for a while, then all of a sudden there you were, on stage at that Wiccaman festival thing. And I started screaming, "*I know her, I know her, she's in my class!*"'

And that's pretty much how the whole morning goes, with everyone wanting to know if I've got a record deal now, and what was it like meeting Phoenix Macleod, and is he as gorgeous in real life as he is on telly – he is. Oh, and do I have his mobile number.

'Actually I'm sort of surprised he didn't give you it,' Cordelia teases as we bundle into Miss Cassidy's art class before lunch. 'I mean he was pretty smitten. He even dedicated that song to you, y'know, the one about falling in love with a crazy girl –'

'OMIGAWD!' Sindi-Sue shrieks like an overexcited parakeet. 'Did he really? Sassy Wilde, I am SO-O-O jealous!'

'Phoenix just said that to please the crowd,' I laugh, even as a little voice inside my head surprises me by whispering, *What if he didn't, Sassy? What if he meant it?* 'In any case,' I add quickly, 'I'm Twig's girlfriend now.'

Then we're all jostling to grab our half-finished papier-mâché projects from the shelf at the back of the room. Megan grabs clumsily for hers and accidentally knocks Tas's sculpture over.

'Do you mind!' Tas mutters. 'Can't you watch what you're doing?'

'Sorry, Tas,' Megan apologizes, immediately bending to pick it up and wipe the dust from it. With an irritated sigh Tas takes it from Megan and turns away.

I'm puzzled. Tas is normally so kind and under-standing. 'Are you OK?' I ask as we pull our art aprons on.

'Course I am,' she says miserably. 'Just a bit tired after the festival, that's all. I didn't sleep well last night.'

'Me neither!' Sindi-Sue exclaims as she tips some paste into a pot. 'I had this dream about me and Phoenix Macleod. We were getting married. A pink fairy-tale wedding with a glass carriage, six white horses, big meringue dress, the works. Oh, Sassy, I can't believe you actually MET him!' She goes all swoony. 'He has such totally gorgeous eyes . . .'

'You can forget about Phoenix Macleod's gorgeous eyes for the next forty minutes,' Miss Cassidy interrupts. 'We need to get these finished so we can paint them next week.'

Obediently we get stuck into tearing up news-paper strips and dipping them in gunge. From time to time I glance across at Tas. When I think about it, she hasn't been herself all morning. She ran into registration at the last minute, then at break time she disappeared to the library. I guess there's something wrong. But then again she was on great form at the Wiccaman festival, so I can't think what.

'Sheesh! I hate Mondays,' Megan yawns after a while. 'A whole week of boring old school stretching ahead. I can't wait for next weekend.'

'That reminds me,' I say. 'Next Friday's sleepover's at my place. Mum asked if we want any DVDs ordered from her club.'

Cordelia looks up from her flying-bat sculpture. 'You know me, Sass,' she grins. '*Night of the Restless Dead . . . Zombies on the Prowl . . . Voodoo Vampires . . .* That kind of thing always makes me happy. But hey, if everyone else wants something different, that's cool.'

I look expectantly at Tas. Tas is an all-singing, all-dancing blockbuster Bollywood romance addict. There's a new one just out – *Moonstruck in Mumbai* – and I know she's desperate to see it.

But she says nothing.

What's more, she's making an absolute mess of her artwork! Just slopping the paste on any old way. She's even got some gunge in her hair. Tas is so NOT your gunge-in-the-hair kinda gal. It can't just be that she didn't sleep well. Even a tired Tas is a tidy Tas.

'What about you, Megan? What DVDs would

you like?' I ask, as I wonder if maybe I can catch Tas alone at lunchtime and find out what's up.

Megan looks surprised. 'Oh,' she says. 'Me? I didn't know I was invited.'

'Well, I did,' Cordelia giggles. 'But I suppose that's cos I'm psychic!'

Playfully, I flick a bit of paste at Cordelia. She ducks, it misses . . . and splats the back of Magnus's head! Fortunately Miss Cassidy's too busy trying to unstick Mad Midge Murphy[3] from his flying saucer creation to notice. Magnus spins round angrily, but when he realizes I'm the culprit, he smiles like I just hit him with one of Cupid's little love arrows. Honestly! Boys are WEIRD!

'Course you're invited, Megan!' I say and Megan's face lights up. 'Only thing is, my room's not that big, so I'm warning you now – four of us will be a bit of a squash.'

'No, it won't,' Taslima blurts. 'Cos I . . . I won't be there.'

We all turn and stare at her.

'Why not?' I ask, confused.

Tas sighs heavily and hangs her head, her dark hair falling across her face. 'I'd like to be there. I really would . . . . But it's my mum . . . . She . . .'

---

[3] Midge claims he's descended from leprechauns on his dad's side. Which, Tas says, would explain his restricted growth. And his inability to keep out of trouble.

Tas hesitates, like she can't find the right words, and I'm hoping it's not gonna be something horrible, like her mum has cancer or is divorcing her dad, or wants to move back to Pakistan or something.

'I'm sorry, Sass . . .' she says quietly. 'Mum says we can't be friends any more.'

Sometimes I get so angry I feel like the top of my head's going to blow right off and flames will come shooting out. Other times I feel so hurt I want to curl up like a distressed porcupine and stick out all my needles to stop anyone coming near.

When Taslima tells me WHY her mum says we can't be friends any more, I don't know whether to explode like a volcano or curl up and crawl away and lick my wounds.

In a small voice Tas explains how her mum saw the clip of me on the TV news on Saturday night while we were all at the festival, and how it was followed up with shots of half-naked men and women drinking and dancing around bonfires on the beach.

'So by the time I got home on Sunday Mum had worked herself into a right tizz,' Tas says miserably. 'She said she would never have let me go to the festival if she'd known it was going to be so wild.'

'But it was, like, totally civilized! We didn't see any of that!' Megan exclaims.

'Yeah, try telling my mother! I told her we were with Sassy's mum the whole time, but she wouldn't listen. She said she saw Sassy with her own eyes, up on stage with hardly a stitch on, and that if she was going to behave like that now she's "a *pop star*", then I couldn't be her friend any more.'

'But didn't she hear what I said before I sang?' I gasp. 'Didn't she understand there was a whole point to the way I was . . . er . . . dressed?'

Tas sighs heavily. 'She was watching with the sound off.'

Poor Taslima. Apparently she pleaded with her mum and argued that it was totally unreasonable to say we couldn't be friends any more.

'In the end I stormed off to my room in tears,' Tas continues, 'and Mum shouted after me, "You see what I mean, Taslima. I told you that girl's been a bad influence. There you go, throwing tantrums now, like a spoiled two-year-old!"'

Half-heartedly I paste a strip of sodden paper on to my sculpture as my mind tries to process everything Tas has just said.

'I'm sorry, Sass,' Taslima says, her bottom lip quivering. 'Mum worries, you know, about me doing well at school. Plus my aunt in Pakistan phoned yesterday, going on and on about how wonderful my cousin Aisya's doing. How she's very serious and always studying. How she's going to get a scholarship to university –'

'But you're the cleverest person we know!' Cordelia exclaims. 'You always do your school-work.'

'Yeah, well, Mum worries I'll not get good enough grades to be a dentist –'

'A dentist?' Cordelia interrupts. 'But you don't want to be a dentist! You want to be a psychologist!'

'I know, I know . . .' Tas groans. 'Mum wants me to be a dentist cos that's what she wanted to do.' She pauses. 'But I really can't stand the thought of poking about in people's mouths . . .' Tas's eyes fill with tears and I forget all my anger.

'Being a chiropodist would be even worse, wouldn't it?' Megan chips in, and everyone turns to look at her. I throw her a grateful look for taking the heat off Tas. 'Imagine having to clip old men's toenails! Gross or what?'

'Or working in Meaty MacBurgers or a butcher's! I would HATE that,' I add, and Tas smiles shakily through her tears. 'I mean, that has to be a vegetarian's nightmare!'

'What about being an undertaker?' Midge Murphy chips in as he reaches across to grab my paste pot. 'All that hanging about in graveyards. Gruesome!'

'Oh, I don't know . . .' Cordelia runs her black-nailed fingers under the tap to wash the glue off. 'I might quite like that actually.'

'Cordelia!' I exclaim, just as the bell goes. 'You

are seriously spooky! I couldn't think of a worse job!'

'I could!' shouts Miss Cassidy as we all chuck our paste-splattered pots towards the sink and dash for the door. 'Art teacher to you lot! Look at the mess I'm left with!'

Outside in the corridor I link arms with Taslima. 'So . . . we're still friends?' she asks quietly.

'Course we are, Tas. Sooner or later your mum will realize I'm *not* the awful empty-headed person she thinks I am; then we can get back to the way things were before.'

'But she's so stubborn, Sass,' Taslima sighs. 'I don't know what it would take to make her see sense.'

'Don't worry, I'll think of something.' I try to smile as we head for the dining hall.

Though, to be honest, right at this moment, I don't have a clue what on earth that something might be.

3

Isn't it strange how some days at school seem to go past in the blink of a gnat's eye, while others go on forever? Today has been a total dddddrrrrrrraaaa-aaaaaaaaaaaaaaaaaaaaaaaaaaaaaaaaaaaaaaaag.

But it's over now. I have served my time, done my penance, suffered greatly, thought up three thousand ways to get into Tas's mum's good books, rejected three thousand ways to get into Tas's mum's good books, spent endless hours wondering if Y-Generation have called yet to offer me a record deal, and now at last, like a kidnap victim who has been incarcerated for years and endured unspeakable torture[4], I emerge blinking into the glorious sunshine.

As Cordelia and me wander across the playground Twig waves from the school wall and my heart lifts.

'Try not to worry about the Tas thing,' Cordelia

---

[4] A double maths

says, giving me a reassuring hug. It will probably all blow over. Parentals are always coming up with big heavy-handed THOU SHALT NOT rules, then they forget all about them a couple of days later. The ageing brain's an amazing thing. A bit like a sieve. Stuff falls through it all the time, never to be seen again.'

'Fun day?' Twig asks, jumping on to his skateboard and rolling along beside me.

'Not really,' I sigh. He listens as I tell him all about Tas and how her mum saw the clip on TV and got totally the wrong end of the stick.

'But Tas's mum can't stop you being friends at school, can she?' Twig asks as he weaves around a lamp post.

'I guess not,' I smile. 'Anyway, how come you still don't go to school? You moved in with Megan and her mum weeks ago now.'

Twig zigzags round a small boy on a bike. 'School's bad for my health. Come out in a horrible rash all over, you know, like a nut allergy. Start wheezing, get that anaphylactic shock thing, go into total meltdown!'

Then he leaps off the board in front of me, flicks it up and catches it.

'Well, *I'm* allergic to school too,' I laugh. 'But I'm MADE to go.'

'Yeah, there have been quite a few letters from the education department asking Dad to get me enrolled,' Twig admits, falling into step beside me. 'But I stick them through the shredder before he gets home . . .'

Just then a butterfly flutters by and lands on a flower. Twig drops his skateboard and creeps up on it. Carefully he catches it in his cupped hands and brings it over to me.

'You know how some people keep butterflies in jars?' Twig says. 'Well, if I had to go to school, it would be like putting a butterfly in a jar.' He opens his hands and the butterfly flutters off into a nearby garden. 'Or,' he says, jumping on his skateboard again, 'a dolphin in a bathtub . . .' Laughing, he powers off the kerb, into the road, curves round a couple of parked cars and flips back up on to the pavement.

'See?' He grins as he slowly circles me. 'I'm a free spirit. I can't be pinned down. Gotta keep moving.'

When we get to my house there's no one in, so the first thing I do is check the phone for messages. Twig stands beside me in the hall, his fingers crossed, his arms crossed, his legs crossed, oh, and his eyes crossed.

'My toes are crossed too,' he grins.

But there's nothing from Y-Generation.

We're in the kitchen grabbing some munchies when Mum comes in, laden with shopping.

'You didn't take any calls for me before you went

out?' I ask anxiously as I slab some peanut butter on an oatcake, top it with a jalapeño and hand it to Twig.

'Sorry, sweetie,' Mum smiles. 'Not a squeak. But here, this came in the post for you.'

She takes a picture postcard from the jumble of mail on the worktop and passes it to me. It's a photo of a field full of colourful tents with an open-air stage in the distance. Across the bottom it says *WICCAMAN FESTIVAL*, and someone's drawn a stick figure with a guitar on the stage and printed *SASSY* above it.

Puzzled, I turn it over. As I scan the message my heart flutters against my ribs.

Hi Sassy!
It was great meeting you and your friends.
Sorry I didn't catch you before you left.
   Hope we can meet again sometime soon.
PHOENIX x.

'Cool card,' says Twig through a mouthful of peanut butter and oatcake. 'Who's it from?'

'It's from Phoenix. Phoenix Macleod.' I say, trying desperately to appear casual even as my heart leaps up and down like an excited two-year-old on a trampoline. 'So, what do you want to drink?' I open the fridge door and start pulling out cartons and bottles. 'Milk? Lemonade? Fruit juice? Smoothie?'

Twig looks at me like I'm mad and pops the last bit of oatcake in his mouth.

I shut the fridge door and grab the kettle. 'Peppermint tea?' I'm totally struggling to cover up the fact that I'm thrilled that Phoenix thought to send me a card. After all, Twig is my official boyfriend and he's totally adorable. The last thing I want is for him to be upset and think I've been flirting with Phoenix.

'Are you . . . OK?' Twig pushes his flop of hair back and fixes me with a curious look.

'Look, that card from Phoenix. I didn't know he was going to send it.' I pour the juice too fast into a glass and it splashes all over the worktop. 'I don't even know how he got my address. I mean, you're my boyfriend . . .' My voice trails off as something tells me I'm not making things any better.

Twig looks at me, puzzled. But puzzled-amused. Not puzzled-angry. 'Yeah, and you're my girl-friend.' He shakes his head and his hair flops over his eyes. 'And it's not a problem if you get postcards from other people . . . It's not actually my business. We don't own each other, do we?'

'Course not,' I say sheepishly. 'But I thought it might . . . you know, bother you.'

'Well, it doesn't.' Twig smiles. And suddenly all my confusion seems well, silly. If it doesn't bother Twig, then why should it bother me? I make a show of pinning Phoenix's card up on the kitchen noticeboard – like it's been sent to the whole family, and not just me.

In any case, I tell myself as Twig and me wander out to the garden to sit in the sun and finish our munchies, Phoenix is just a cool chico I met once-upon-a-time at a festival.

Chances are I'll never see or hear from him again.

4

It's Thursday and I STILL haven't heard from Y-Generation. I was starting to get seriously worried they'd forgotten all about me, but in maths Cordelia said she sneaked a peek in her mum's crystal ball last night and she saw a Y-Generation car parked at my front door and Ben and Zing getting out. 'I can't say exactly *when* they're gonna turn up,' she explained as we copied the answers to some algebraic equations from Tas's jotter. 'But I saw it REALLY clearly. So they're bound to call sometime soon.' So that's cheered me up quite a lot.

Which is good, cos I'm pretty upset about the whole Taslima thing. All week she's been unnaturally[5] quiet. Cordelia and me have been doing our best to act totally upbeat and chatty around her, but NOTHING has made her smile. Not even

---

[5] Tas is always quiet – so *unnaturally* quiet is a pretty freaky state.

Mad Midge Murphy doing his impersonation of Arizona Kelly's latest video – you know the one, where she pretends she's a wild cat locked in a cage – and kinda sounds like one too.

When the bell for lunchtime goes, Tas slips out before the rest of us have even packed our bags.

'Where's Tas gone?' I ask as Megan, Cordelia and me push and shove our way along the busy corridor to the lunch hall. 'Do you think she's OK?'

'Uh oh,' says Megan, throwing a look at Cordelia. 'Hasn't she told you?'

'Told me what?'

'That she's joined Maths Club,' Cordelia says. 'So she won't be spending Thursday lunchtimes with us now.'

'And that's not all –' Megan adds eagerly, as I choose a cheese and chutney baguette from the fridge display. 'She's joining Chess Club on Fridays too, and Silent Reading Club on Wednesdays.'

'But she doesn't even like chess! And if she goes to all the lunchtime clubs I'll hardly see her at all!' I splutter.

Cordelia sticks her thumb on the infrared reader to pay for her pizza slice. 'I think her mum's behind all these lunchtime club things. She's trying to make sure Tas sees as little of us as possible.'

'As little of *me* as possible, you mean,' I mutter. 'This is SO unfair! Oh, Cordelia, surely there must be something I can do to make Mrs Ankhar change her mind about me?'

'Yeah, there is,' Cordelia says as she slurps her bat's-blood juice. 'Give up singing, dedicate yourself to your studies, sign up to Maths and Chess Club and decide to be a dentist. Then she'll think you're a perfect friend for Taslima.'

Twig's waiting for me after school again, and – YAY! – this time he's NOT brought his skateboard like he did on Monday and Tuesday, or his bike like he did yesterday, which means we might even get round to HOLDING HANDS on the way home like a real boyfriend and girlfriend!

'I've found this great website where you can sign up to petitions protesting against cruelty to animals,' Twig says as we wander along the path at the edge of Bluebell Wood.

'Sounds cool.' I edge closer to him so we're almost bumping shoulders. My free hand accidentally brushes his and I'm thinking I'll maybe just GRAB his hand – when suddenly he breaks into a sprint! Seconds later he's on top of the high stone wall that edges the pavement.

'Yeah,' he shouts down, like it's the most natural thing in the world that his feet are now level with my eyes. 'I'll send you the link. Animals can't speak for themselves, so it's important we speak up for them.'

Then he leaps from the wall, cartwheels twice

and lands, his arms wide like an Olympic gymnast, in front of me.

'Very good. Twelve out of ten,' I smile. Cos hey, maybe Twig doesn't quite get the hand-holding thing, but he does know how to surprise me!

When we get to my house Brewster's dozing on the front door step. As soon as Twig sees him he drops to his knees and fusses over him. Happily, Brewster rolls over on to his back to get his tummy tickled. Hmmphh, old Brewster's getting more attention than me[6], I think ruefully as I chuck my ruckie towards the coat stand, and I'm about to go into the kitchen to ask Mum if there's been any message yet from Y-Generation when Dad comes rushing out of his office.

'Sassy! At last!' he says, all excited.

I hold my breath – and wait for him to say that Y-Generation has called. Instead he holds up a banana-coloured waistcoat thing studded with reflectors, and a fluorescent bike helmet with a flashing light like a radioactive lemon stuck on top. It's totally ridiculous.

I look at my dad in horror. 'What is *that*?'

'It's new safety gear – part of a government drive to improve the safety of teen cyclists,' he prattles.

'And we would like *you*,' Digby, Dad's assistant,

---

[6] Not that I want my tummy tickled! No way!

chips in, his face shiny with enthusiasm, 'to cycle to school every day next week wearing it –'

'To make it seem cool and trendy,' Dad adds eagerly.

I cast a horrified eye over the waistcoat. Not only is it shapeless, it's made from some atrocious shiny nylon stuff.

'Go on, Sassy. Try it on. Let's see what it looks like,' Dad urges.

'Count me out on this one, Dad. No one could make that stuff look trendy.'

'I can make it worth your while.' Dad follows me into the kitchen. Honestly! He used to be quite straightforward, but now he's a politician he thinks nothing of using bribery and corruption to get his way.

'Dad,' I say patiently as I chop a kiwi and pop it in the smoothie-maker with some ice, 'you can't buy me off. I don't need your help in getting a demo disc any more.'

'Yeah.' Pip dances through the kitchen with a tiny hamster clinging for dear life to her shoulder. 'Sassy's got her own recording deal now.'

'Well, not quite yet. Did Y-Generation call today?' I toss in a handful of frozen berries and a dollop of ice cream. 'I mean, if they don't hurry up I'm probably going to have a nervous break-down from all the stress of waiting –'

'No, I'm afraid not . . .' Dad looks sympathetic

for a moment, then brightens. 'So that means I can still bribe you!' He dangles the cycle waistcoat in front of me.

'No way! I have my image to look after.' I press the button and the blender pulverizes the fruit. 'I mean, what if the paparazzi caught me in that hideous outfit?' I shout above the din.

He doesn't get the chance to answer, cos guess what? The doorbell rings. I dash through to the living room and peer out the window. A Y-Generation car's parked outside – exactly as Cordelia predicted!

'HOLY GUACAMOLE!' I shout. 'It's Ben and Zing!'

Just then the old grandfather clock in the hall chimes, Brewster starts barking and Mum shouts from the living room, 'I'm on the phone can some-one get the door please!'

I'm already there, Twig on my heels, my whole future flashing in front of me, my heart thumping. This is it. At last, Sassy Wilde, aged thirteen and a bit, is about to get her big break!

5

As I open the door for Ben and Zing I swear I am just one ginormous quivering lump of jelly.

Fortunately, Mum finishes her phone call and takes control, ushering everyone into the kitchen. We sit at the big pine table in exactly the same seats we sat on when Ben and Zing came to offer me the chance of making a demo disc a few weeks back. I can hardly believe that so much has happened in such a short space of time! Twig stands quietly by the window. Dad and Digby come through. And Pip, her hamster now cradled carefully in her hand, perches on a bar stool.

Then there's a silence. A big, heavy, awkward silence.

Ben clears his throat, but even before he says anything I know I'm not going to like what I hear. It's like he's got a banner hanging above his head with *BAD NEWS* written in big bold letters.

'I might as well get straight to the point,' Ben

says. 'I'm sorry, Sassy. Y-Generation have decided not to sign you.'

For a minute I think he's actually said, 'Y-Generation are delighted to sign you.' But I know that's just my stupid brain clutching at straws. Then it's like I'm falling under water, sinking, sinking, bubbles rushing up past my ears.

'We really, really are sorry.' Zing's voice echoes as if from far away. 'We did our best to convince the Board of Directors. We told them how brilliant you were at the Wiccaman festival, how you electrified the crowd.'

I sink my teeth into my bottom lip to stop the tears coming.

'We did our best,' Ben repeats softly. 'We really did, Sass.'

Mum stops making coffee and comes over and puts an arm round me. Digby slips quietly from the room. Twig looks shocked.

'So what happened? I mean . . . why not? I don't understand . . .' I stammer, the tears brimming over and streaming down my cheeks. Silently Pip passes her hamster to Twig and comes over and wraps her arms round me too.

Ben sighs heavily. 'It was Paradiso's. They blocked it.'

'Paradiso's?' Mum gasps. 'What have Paradiso's got to do with who *you* sign?'

'They're one of Y-Generation's biggest outlets,'

Zing explains. 'If Paradiso's won't stock our CDs, then we go under.'

'And they were so furious with Sassy's attack on them at the Wiccaman festival,' Ben continues, 'that's what they were threatening to do. Sassy accused Paradiso's of using child labour, on national TV. It was seen by millions.'

'Yeah, even Taslima's mum saw it,' Twig mutters quietly.

'So that's it, Sassy. I'm sorry, but Y-Generation simply can't afford to sign you. We'd be risking the whole company if we did.' Zing's voice is business-like. 'We didn't want to let you know by phone. We felt we should at least come in person. We know it must be a huge disappointment.'

Ben stands and takes his car keys from his pocket. 'I'd like you to know, Mr and Mrs Wilde, that I think your daughter has a huge talent. What's more I think she's a great kid. If there was any way I could help get her music out there, believe you me – I'd do it. But I can't see what can be done. I'm sorry.'

Ben squeezes my shoulder as he leaves.

'Never mind, love,' Dad says supportively. 'I'm sure there are other recording companies –'

'Look, I hope you don't think it's cruel of me to say this, Mr Wilde,' Zing says quietly as she goes to follow Ben out, 'but it's probably best you don't hold out false hopes. If a huge organization like Paradiso's has blacklisted Sassy, then no other company's going to come near. I'm sorry, Sassy. Realistically there's nowhere you can go from here.'

I feel Mum stiffening. 'I'll show you out,' she says coldly.

The phone rings and Dad goes to answer it. Twig looks at me.

'I'm really, really sorry,' he says, his face pale.

I open my mouth to speak. I want to be brave, say it doesn't matter, it was just a recording deal, that I'm glad I made my stand against people who use child labour, that I know I did the right thing, I can hold my head high – but the words won't come. Instead a big sob surges up and out of my mouth. Distraught, I turn on my heel, stumble up to my room and slam the door.

As I throw myself on to my bed and shove my face into the pillow, all my disappointment floods out, unstoppable, like an angry river that's burst its banks. My whole body shakes and sobs and hurts.

This is so unfair! All I ever try to do is the right thing!

So why, oh why, oh why does everyone think I'm trouble?

6

As the sound of Ben and Zing's car fades into the distance, my dreams and hopes fade with them.

After a few minutes Mum taps gently on my room door. 'Sassy, can I come in?'

I make a snuffly noise into the pillow. It means *Go away and leave me alone to die, please,* but obviously Mum doesn't understand sob-language, cos next minute she's sitting on the edge of my bed, smoothing my hair.

'Are you OK, honey?' Mum's voice is soft.

I shake my head without looking up. With a heave Mum hoists dear old Brewster up on to the bed beside me. Still sobbing into my pillow, I stretch out an arm and pull him close.

Then Mum shuts the bedroom curtains, picks my favourite fleecy blanket up from the floor and tucks it over me.

'I'll be downstairs if you need me,' Mum whispers into my hair. 'I know it's a big disappointment, but there's sure to be a way round it. There always is.'

As she leaves she quietly closes the door. Brewster

snuggles into me like he really understands, and licks the tears from my face with his rough tongue.

That night I don't go down for dinner. I can't.

Eventually Dad brings up a big mug of tea and a salad sandwich. But I'm way too distraught to eat, so I leave them sitting on the bedside table till the tea grows a milky film on top and the bread curls at the edges.

After a while I hear a tapping on my window. I guess Twig's climbed up into the branches outside.

'Sassy,' says Twig's voice. 'It's me. . . can I come in?'

'I don't want to see anyone.' With all the sobbing my voice kinda croaks and I'm not sure whether or not he hears.

A few minutes pass and I'm wondering if he's still there, when he starts playing a tune on his tin whistle – a melancholy tune that matches exactly the way I feel – and as I listen, one final little tear seeps out of the corner of my eye and trickles down my cheek.

Then he plays a silly lively tune where he keeps hitting the wrong notes. I've never heard Twig hit wrong notes before and my brain knows he's doing it to try to make me smile. But I can't. My heart is frozen solid.

'I'm going to stay out here till you open your curtains,' Twig's voice calls after a while. Then he starts playing again and before I know it, I drift off to sleep . . .

*

When I wake, the room's full of shadows. I glance at the clock – 9.15. For a wonderful moment I think it's morning! That Ben and Zing's visit has been no more than a bad dream. Then I realize it's 9.15 IN THE EVENING. There was no bad dream. The visit was real . . . and I feel worse than ever.

I drag myself over to the window, open the curtains a chink and stare into the green leaves outside. But Twig's gone. And I can't say I blame him. As I pad back across my room I catch a glimpse of myself in the mirror. A wreck of a girl, with greasy hair, a blotchy face, red-rimmed eyes. Unhappily I throw myself on to the bed. It was a mistake ever to think I could be anyone's girlfriend. I should call Twig right now. Tell him he doesn't have to be my boyfriend any more. That he's free to find himself someone else. Someone who's fun to be around. Someone with a future.

And I'm just thinking I might become a recluse and take a vow of silence and never leave my room again, when somewhere in the rumple of my duvet my mobile starts ringing. Of course, when I eventually detect it, it stops. Then almost immediately a text message pings in: Ben told me. Y-Gen r FOOLS! So so sorry, Sassy. Spk soon. Phoenix :o(xxx

As I read, my heart – which I honestly thought was dead – flutters.

Then another text pings in: Anything I can do - just ask. P x

My little bird of a heart lifts its head and opens one eye . . . as another text pings in: It would be good to see you soon . . .x

My heart staggers to its feet, and despite myself I feel a smile twitch at the corners of my mouth.

Troubled, I flump back on my pillows. How come a text message from Phoenix Macleod is the only thing that makes me feel alive again?!

Just then the phone in the hall rings and – can you believe it? – for a split second my treacherous heart hopes it will be Phoenix calling on the land-line. There's a clatter as Pip skips through from the living room, then her phone-answering voice chirps, 'This is the Wilde residence. Philippa Wilde, model, actress and all-round-highly-talented person speaking. How can I help you?'

Next minute she thunders upstairs and bursts into my room. 'It's Cordelia,' she says breathlessly as she pushes the cordless phone into my hand. 'She knows everything.' And before I can protest that I'm not taking any calls, Pip disappears.

With a sigh I put the phone to my ear.

'Listen, you don't have to explain,' Cordelia says quickly.[7] 'But if there's anything I can do, just ask.'

'Thanks,' I whisper hoarsely. 'I guess I'll be fine.'

'So what about school tomorrow? Do you think you'll make it?' Cordelia's voice is full of concern.

[7] How on earth did she know I was there? Freaky!

'I just want to stay in bed for a while,' I sniff. 'Like three thousand years or something. So no, I won't be at school.'

'What about tomorrow's sleepover?' Cordelia asks.

'I'd really rather not. I just want to be on my own for a while.'

'No probs,' Cordelia says. 'Don't worry about a thing. Remember we're your bezzies. We don't care about record deals and we'll never buy any Y-Generation CDs again. Or shop at Paradiso's. And Sassy –' she pauses. 'Don't ask me how I know this . . . but things aren't as bad as you think. They're gonna work out OK. I've got this gut feeling about it, y'know?'

I say bye to Cordelia, then set the phone on my bedside table and lie and stare at the ceiling. After a while I pick it up again. Cos I figure Cordelia's right. Bezzies should always be there for you. And right now more than anything I need to talk to Taslima. She always knows how to make me feel better when I'm at my lowest. In any case, as I'm not going to be a 'pop star' now, Mrs Ankhar can't have a problem with me any more, can she?

Quickly I punch in Taslima's number.

'Hello?' says Mrs Ankhar's voice.

'Can I speak to Taslima, please?' I say extra-super-politely.

'Who is this?'

I take a deep breath. 'It's Sassy.'

'Taslima can't come to the phone right now,' Mrs Ankhar says sharply. 'And I'm waiting for an important call, so please don't call back.'

AND THEN SHE HANGS UP!

I stare at the phone in disbelief. Only last week my life was so GOOD. I was on track for making it as a singer, I had a brand-new boyfriend and two brilliant best buds. And now? Now everything is spoiled. I've lost Taslima, I'm all muddled up about Twig and Phoenix, and I've blown my one chance at a record deal.

Honestly! My life is in TATTERS. And there's NOTHING I can do to make it any better.

All night Dad snores like an orang-utan with a bad cold, Houdini spins furiously in his hamster wheel, Brewster whimpers in his sleep like he's having scary dreams, the owl in Bluebell Wood hoots . . . and I lie awake.

As dawn breaks, soft shadows creep slowly across the ceiling, until eventually sunlight filters through the curtains and the room fills with colour.

At half past eight Mum brings me a smoothie made with all my fave fruits. 'Your dad made this for you specially,' she says, her face all worried. She hands me a fancy stemmed glass with half a strawberry decorating the rim. I take a sip. It tastes sour and horrible.

'I can't get up, Mum,' I whisper. 'I can't face anyone. Not yet. And I feel sick. Really sick. I can't go to school. I don't want to see anyone. So can I stay in bed? Please?'

Frowning, Mum puts a hand on my brow. 'I suppose you do look tired and a bit pale . . .'

'Just today?' I plead.

Mum takes a deep breath. 'You promise you'll go back to school on Monday? No nonsense?'

I nod my head vigorously.

'OK, sweetie.' She smoothes my hair. 'Have a quiet day today. I know this has all been a big shock and disappointment. You'll feel much better tomorrow.'

'Mum,' I sniff. 'Last night you said I'd feel better tomorrow. But now today *is* last night's tomorrow – and guess what? I don't feel better at all.'

I turn over and push my face into the pillow. With some luck I'll fall asleep and suffocate. And why? Cos not only am I miserable and a loser, but now I'm HORRIBLE too. Mum was being lovely to me, and what did I do? I told her a WHOPPING GREAT BIG LIE.

I have no intention of going to school on Monday. In fact, if I don't accidentally wake up dead – which is my preferred option – I might never leave my room again.

7

Friday morning drags on forever. But I don't care. I may as well face up to it. This is what the rest of my life is going to be like. If I can't sing, there's no point in me doing anything. It's the only thing I was ever good at.

Pip's at school and Mum's gone out to help her mad hippy friend Cathy who's opened The Totally Scrumptious Cake Cafe in the town centre. She says she should be back by early afternoon. Dad and Digby have gone to visit the factory that's making the new cycle safety gear. (Hopefully they've realized they'll never get young people to wear safety waistcoats and helmets if they make them look like extras from a spoof alien film.)

Normally if I have some time on my own I spend it playing guitar and writing songs. But I won't be doing that again now. Ever.

I stare at my guitar. It stares back. And I'm just thinking about what to do with it – like dig a big hole in the back garden and bury it, or build a ceremonial funeral pyre and set it alight – when the doorbell rings. DING *DING* DONG!

Pointedly I ignore it. But then it rings again. DING *DING* DONG And this time it just keeps going. *DING DING DONG DING DING DONG!*

'OK, OK, OK!' I mutter, tugging on my dressing gown and slobbing downstairs. I open the front door a crack and I'm about to explain there's no one at home, just miserable little me and since I've got TERMINAL DEPRESSION and it's HIGHLY CONTAGIOUS it's probably better to leave IMMEDIATELY – when my jaw drops open.

'Taslima!' I exclaim, dragging her inside before anyone spots her and reports her to school. 'I tried to call you last night but your mum hung up! And I really wanted to speak to you, cos . . .'

'Sassy, I –' Taslima begins.

'Oh, don't say anything, Tas,' I blurt as she follows me into the kitchen. 'Everything's such a mess. I don't know what I'm going to do –'

'Sassy!' Taslima interrupts. 'Can you stop talking about yourself . . . just for a minute . . . please?'

I stare at her, open-mouthed. Tas is usually so sympathetic!

'I came round cos something awful's happened.' She sinks on to a kitchen chair. 'In Pakistan. Where Mum's family are. There's been a huge earthquake. Mum spent all last night trying to get in touch with the Pakistani Embassy, but it's hard to get any info cos the phones are down.'

'Oh, Tas, I'm really, really sorry.' My brain whirrs as it catches up with what Taslima is saying.

'Mum told me this morning you'd phoned,' Tas sighs heavily. 'She doesn't know I'm here, but I had to see you . . .' Her voice trails off as she tries not to break down.

'Are Aisya and her family OK?' I ask quietly. Tas and her big sis, Jamila, went on holiday to Pakistan last summer. They stayed with Aisya and brought back tons of photos.

Taslima shakes her head. 'We don't know. We can't get any news. Mum's village is right in the middle of where the earthquake hit. That's why I'm not at school. Mum's decided to go to Pakistan to find them. We're leaving first thing tomorrow –'

'What?' I ask, aghast. 'You're going to Pakistan? But you can't, Tas. I mean, isn't it still dangerous?'

Taslima looks at me, her face pale, her eyes gleaming with tears. 'Jamila's got her finals at uni, and I can't let Mum go on her own. She gets in such a tizz about planes and travel. She'd never cope. And we don't know what she's going to find when she gets there.' Taslima's voice wobbles as I follow her to the front door. 'I didn't want to leave without seeing you. But, listen, I have to go . . . Mum's so upset already. She's not good with stress. She'd freak if she knew I was here. But I didn't want you to think I'd just gone off. You must be totally cut up about the record deal.'

'Oh, Tas,' I say, hugging her. 'The record deal doesn't matter. Not really. And I'll always be your friend. You know that.'

Tas sniffs and I feel her head nodding. 'I'll miss you,' she whispers into my hair.

'I'll miss you too.' I say as she pulls herself away. 'Be careful, Tas.'

As I stand in the doorway and watch as she hurries away, thoughts crowd my head. Thoughts of how sweet and brave Taslima is. Of how awful it must be to know your family's caught up in a disaster halfway round the world. Of how much I'll miss Tas. How I'll worry about her till she's safely back.

But one big thought dominates. How oh how could I get so upset about a stupid recording deal?

8

I remember hearing Mum say once that you're only given one life, so you have to make sure you live it. I didn't understand that at the time, but I think I do now.

After Tas goes I switch on *News 24*. Live reports are starting to come in from the earthquake area. I pull my dressing gown tight round me as footage of devastated towns and villages floats across the screen. Everything looks grey and dusty. Buildings have crumpled as if made from cardboard. Exhausted people sit in shock in front of fallen houses. Ambulance sirens wail. Workers with shovels and pickaxes risk their lives trying to help the trapped and the injured.

And that's when it hits me. I am so lucky to be alive! OK, so no way am I ever going to sing again – Y-Generation and Paradiso's have seen to that – but there must still be tons of other things I can do with my life. From here on in I'm going to practise **POSITIVE THINKING**.

I switch the TV off and swing into action. First I leap into the shower and let the hot water run over my shoulders and wash all the gallons of self-pity I've been wallowing in down the plughole.

Back in my room, as I open my wardrobe door to get some clothes, my hand brushes against the lovely purple shirt Phoenix gave me at the Wiccaman festival. I remember the text messages I got last night and how much they cheered me up. *Go on, Sassy, put Phoenix's shirt on*, a little voice says inside my head. *It will make you feel better. You know it will.*

But no! I tell that little voice it is WRONG. It was sweet of Phoenix to send those texts, but I absolutely cannot wear Phoenix's shirt while I'm Twig's girlfriend. So I take a deep breath and shove the shirt into the darkest corner, behind old tops and jackets I've not worn for years, then I pull out a clean Tee and shorts and slam the wardrobe door shut.

By the time I head downstairs, Mum's home. 'Honey!' she beams as I bounce into the kitchen. 'It's great to see you up and showered. That smoothie you didn't want this morning's in the fridge. Would you like it now?'

'Thanks, Mum,' I say and give her a hug.

And guess what? When I taste the smoothie it's not bitter in the slightest. It's lovely. In fact, it's just the way I like it.

I down the smoothie out on the patio, then sit for a while thinking. Tas once told me that some people go through life moaning that their glass is half empty. Other people think they're lucky cos their glass is half full. But both people have the exact same amount! Tas figures you can choose whether to be happy with the way your life is, or be unhappy with it. I'm still healthy, and my house is still standing and my family are safe, so I guess my glass is at least half full and that's not a bad way to be.

As I count up all the reasons why I'm actually a very lucky person, I wander up to my room and fetch my TOTALLY SECRET NOTEBOOK and a pen.

Moments later, sitting on the old swing at the bottom of the garden, the bees buzzing lazily in the honeysuckle that climbs up over the potting shed, I open the notebook and start writing.

My Resolutions

I know it's not New Year or anything[8], but hey! Today marks a whole new phase in the life of Sassy Wilde. Yesterday I thought I was going to be a singing star, but now it's all over and that is FINAL.

---

[8] Though it probably is somewhere. After all, the Hindu New Year's in March!

Cos today I'm going to be something else.

Just like the caterpillar cannot possibly know when it crawls from the ~~chrystalis~~ ~~chrissalist~~ ~~chrystallist~~ cocoon that it's now turned into a beautiful butterfly, so I do not yet know as I emerge from the wreckage of my singing career what I am actually in fact turning into.

It must be the same, I suppose, for a tadpole. I mean, you spend the first part of your life swimming about thinking, 'Hey, this is fun! I really love having a little ink-blob head and a wiggly tail and playing races with all my little brother and sister tadpoles.' Then you sprout legs and turn green and grow warts and next thing you're hopping about and croaking and catching insects on your tongue.

I score that last bit out after I write it. I prefer the bit before about the butterfly. I wouldn't mind being a butterfly, looking pretty, flitting from flower to flower[9] . . . But imagine going to sleep a tadpole and waking up a toad? Hmmph . . . that would be a bad start to the day.

But to get to the point. I, Sassy Wilde, as of right now this minute, am going to be a totally different person. Life is too short. You never

[9] And maybe even meeting up with a Twig butterfly!

know when something awful might happen. Like an earthquake or a tsunami or a volcano erupting or a meteor hitting the earth or something. Especially with the planet heating up and all the scientists warning us about climate catastrophe and all the politicians messing about and not taking it seriously.

So, as I am fed up with everyone thinking I am TROUBLE and BAD NEWS and only interested in myself, I do hereby faithfully and most ~~solemly solemenly~~ solemnly make the following resolutions:

1. I will do at least five (5) good turns EVERY day.
2. I will be nice and sweet and kind to everyone . . . OK, I suppose that has to include Magnus Menzies.
3. I will NEVER EVER sing again. Instead I will be open-minded about what I should do with my life and I will try out NEW THINGS till I find something I am really really good at which will make my life WORTHWHILE and INTERESTING.

   Signed <u>Sassy Wilde</u>

I snap the notebook shut then run up to my room and I'm tucking it into the back of the drawer in my bedside table when I notice my guitar, still leaning against my desk. A reminder of what might have been. What now will never be. Part of my past. A past I am determined to put behind me forever.

I tug my big black guitar case out of the wardrobe and lay the guitar carefully inside. For a moment it feels like I'm placing it – and my career – in a coffin. I stroke the smooth wood for the last time. Then I quickly close the lid and clip the case shut.

Of course, when I tell Mum what I'm about to do she tries to stop me.

'Can't you just put your guitar up in the attic or something?' she suggests as she looks up from her book, *Cakes to Kill For*. 'Just because Y-Generation don't want to sign you, doesn't mean you have to give up singing completely. Honestly, Sassy, there's no need to throw the baby out with the bathwater!'

'Look, Mum,' I say as I head out the door. 'I'm thirteen. I know what I'm doing. This is my life. I have the right to make my own decisions. My guitar is part of my past now. I want it to be sold for charity. I'm making a fresh start and I really don't think you should be trying to stop me!'

Mum shakes her head and snaps her book shut. 'Why have you always got to go to extremes, Sassy?'

'And why have you always got to treat me like a two-year-old when I am level-headed, balanced and mature!' I explode as I pick up my guitar and flounce out (like a two-year-old) before she can stop me.

As I approach the charity shop I almost lose my nerve. I swear the handle of the case feels like it's superglued to my fingers. I even imagine I can hear my guitar's strings quietly twanging, like it's pleading with me not to give it up for adoption.

Resolutely I look at the posters in the window about the work Oxfam does with the money it raises, like helping street kids who have nothing, and sick babies in drought-stricken countries who need clean water. I think about Tas and how brave she is, going to an area hit by an earthquake to find her relatives. And I *know* I'm doing the right thing.

The woman in the shop is delighted when I hoist the guitar case on to the counter. 'We often get young people looking for a first guitar,' she beams at me as she undoes the clips. 'I don't think they realize it takes a lot of patience. You've really got to work at it.'

'I know. I just couldn't be bothered with all the practice,' I lie.

She opens the case and takes my guitar out. 'Well, it's beautiful. It's sure to be snaffled up by someone who'll have great fun with it.' She strums it gently and tears spring up in my eyes. Quickly I head for the door, a big lump forming in my throat. Outside, I watch as she balances it in the window beside a baby buggy and a rusty old lawnmower. It takes all my strength not to rush back in to say *Sorry, I've changed my mind, can I have it back, please?*

As I walk swiftly away a small voice niggles at me. *You're making a big mistake here, Sassy. You can no more give up singing than you can give up breathing. And you can't do this to your guitar. It's part of your life. Part of your family. You wouldn't give Brewster away, would you? Think of all the good times you had together. Turn round. It's not too late. Get it back!*

I start whistling to drown the little voice out and a *Big Issue* seller standing outside the post office grins at me.

'Someone's in a good mood!' he quips. 'It's a lovely thing to see. There's too much misery in this world. Want to buy a magazine? Help the homeless?'

I've only got enough for my bus fare, but I suppose if I buy a *Big Issue*, then that would make Good Deed Number Two for today. Unfortunately it also means I'll have to walk a couple of miles home – but, I remind myself as I hand the money over, walking is more eco-friendly. The planet will thank me for it.

'Thanks, love,' he smiles. 'God bless.'

As I set off briskly for home I force myself to think of my new life ahead. Maybe I'll be a doctor and, you know, help people caught up in war zones. Or an investigative journalist uncovering scandals and cover-ups by big companies like Paradiso's. Or a charity worker helping build hospitals and schools in Africa. Or a scientist developing a cure for cancer.

See, I tell myself, the possibilities are limitless! I could be an astronaut, or an artist, a footballer, an animator, a vet, a forensic scientist, a psychologist, a psychiatrist, a psychopath[10] – Ha! I could even be a dentist and earn pots of money!

But one thing's for sure, I'm not going to be a singer.

So I'm NEVER going to need a guitar again.

[10] Ooops! Just discovered what that is. Maybe not . . .

9

As soon as I get home I send Twig a quick email to say thanks for being sweet last night and to let him know I'm fine. It takes about three seconds to write the email. And about three hours to decide how to sign off, cos I really don't know how you sign off to a boyfriend.

I try:

Byeee, Sassy ☺

C U soon! Sass x

Lots of love and kisses, Sassy xxx

Luv & Hugs, Sassy W.

Can't wait to see you, S x

Rock the Planet! Sassy xxx

Yours sincerely, Ms Sassy Wilde

In the end I type *S*, decide on one *x*, add another one for good luck, hope that's about right, press Send, and set about continuing with my good deeds.

Mum's in the kitchen baking a pile of sweet little fairy cakes for Cathy's Totally Scrumptious Cake

Cafe, so I explain at length my new philosophy for life and how I am going to be a totally good person now and dedicate myself to helping others. 'So how can I help you?' I ask at last.

'You can't,' Mum takes the tray of cakes from the oven. 'I did the washing-up while you were telling me about how helpful you were going to be. In any case,' she adds as she gives me the cake-mix spoon to lick clean, 'it's a beautiful day, sweetheart. Why not go round and see Cordelia? You've had a tough time – you need to relax!'

'But I don't want to relax!' I protest as I lick the last of the cake mix from the spoon. 'I want to *help* people!'

'OK,' she sighs. 'Your dad's through in the dining room. Maybe he's got letters needing posting or something. Goodness knows, he's up to his eyes in constituency work. I suppose he would appreciate an extra pair of hands.'

Since Dad's election our dining room has become Dad's office. He's assured me and Pip that this is a temporary measure until Digby finds him suitable premises in the town centre. Meanwhile, the dining room's a muddle of files and folders and piles of papers and letters.

'I'm not sure there's anything you can actually do to help,' Digby says, riffling through a mess of correspondence. 'The thing is, the system's a bit chaotic.'

'Digby means *non-existent*,' Dad groans. 'But we're working on it.'

'I suppose you could shred that lot.' Digby points at a big untidy pile of papers and a tiny shredder. 'We're about to run through your dad's diary for the week, so you'll need to be quiet, though.'

'No worries,' I assure him brightly as I settle down in the corner with the shredder. 'I can be very quiet.'

Which is how I find out about the visit to Fossil Grove Old Folks' Home.

'So I'll pick you up at seven on Wednesday and we'll go straight there,' Digby instructs Dad. 'The matron will be waiting to meet you. You'll have tea and cake with some of the younger residents, shake a few hands, have a few photos taken, and then we'll leave.'

'Dad,' I interrupt as a brilliant thought hits me. 'Can I come with you?'

'What?' Dad sounds surprised. 'It's a retirement home, Sassy. Full of old people. You moan if you have to visit your own gran!'

'But I'm a changed person,' I explain patiently as I continue to shred. 'I am practising positive thinking. I want to be kind. I want to help people. There might be an old person I could take out for a spin in their wheelchair or something.'

'I think that's a great idea,' Digby's face lights up. 'Having a lovely bright young person like Sassy along will do the residents no end of good. It would be an excellent PR move.'

Dad looks doubtful, but Digby – bless his little cotton socks – overrules him. I finish shredding the papers and pile all the spaghetti strips into the recycling bin.

'All done,' I say proudly. 'And don't worry about tomorrow, Dad. You'll be glad you let me come along.'

Maybe if I can't be a singer, I should be a politician like my dad. I quite fancy persuading people to stop using so much electricity and buying so many cars and totally overheating the planet.

Which reminds me! I started a letter of complaint months ago, but what with all my excitement over that silly being-a-star stuff, I never got it finished.

In my room I rummage in my desk drawers looking for the letter. It's buried under tons of half-finished song lyrics. I get a momentary pang when I see how many songs I've started. For a split second I think I should maybe have a ceremonial fire out in the garden and burn all the song stuff. After all, I don't have any use for it now, do I? But I worry about the polluting effects of the smoke and how it might contribute to global warming, so I just cram all the bits back in the drawer and force it shut.

Then I stretch out on my rainbow rug and quickly finish my letter to the prime minister of Australia.

33 Anton Drive
Strathcarron

Dear Prime Minister of Australia

Toxic Sheep

It has come to my attention that Australia is full of sheep. As you are no doubt aware, sheep have weird digestive systems that cause them to burp and . . . err . . . release from their bottoms . . . huge amounts of methane into the earth's atmosphere — 90 million tonnes a year, in fact. Methane, in case you did not know, is a pretty awful stinky gas. It contributes hugely to global warming and puts the future of the planet at risk.

No doubt you are elderly yourself and will die soon anyway, so this may not seem like a great big problem to you. But I am still young (see below), and I and my generation would like to have a lovely safe planet to live on once you've popped your clogs.

May I suggest that you tell your Australian farmers they should breed less sheep? In any case they only breed them to kill them. So what is the point?!

Should you insist on keeping your sheep, I think you should seriously consider investing in

new technology to catch the sheep . . . err . . .
emissions and stop them escaping into the air
and killing the rest of us. Scientists in New
Zealand have already invented a sheep-emissions-
catching device, so maybe you could get in touch
with them and find out more?

Please raise this matter as soon as possible
in the Australian Parliament. Oh, and please get
back to me and let me know what you and your
government decide.

Yours sincerely
Sassy Wilde
Aged 13

I borrow a couple of stamps and an envelope from
the piles of stuff in the dining room, copy the
address down from the Internet, then wander out
to the post box at the end of the road.

That's it. Three good deeds completed already!

By teatime I'm feeling miles better. It's amazing
how doing things to help others makes you feel so
good! I cleaned out Pip's hamster cage while she
was out playing and she was incredibly grateful. I
couldn't find any old newspapers for the bottom
cos Mum had just taken them all to the community
recycling bin, but I found some stuff on Digby's
to-be-shredded pile. They were a great fit too.

I didn't even have to fold them like I do with Dad's big newspapers. And Pip was delighted cos they were a particularly pretty shade of pink. 'Pink,' she gushed, 'is Houdini's fave colour. It's excellent rodent feng shui. It creates happy hamster vibes.'

After tea I insist on loading the dishwasher – without anyone telling me to. (Good Deed Number 5!)

'You know, Sassy,' Mum says as she puts her feet up while I clean the cooker, 'I rather like this new version of you.'

10

I have just had the most fantastic insight! When you're cleaning a cooker your brain can work out all sorts of other things. I am elbow-deep in soapy suds, scrubbing the hob rings, when I realize what I have to do to sort out my love life. Instead of splitting up with Twig – that AWFUL thought I had last night when I was stuck right in the middle of my BIG LIFE CRISIS – I will forget about Phoenix, calm my hair down, maybe even put on a smidgeon of make-up, and go round to see Twig to say a big romantic thank you for being so sweet. Who knows, I think mischievously as I take off Mum's rubber gloves and stick them on top of the taps to dry, he might even get round to kissing me!

It's almost eight by the time I'm ready. 'Whooty-whoo!' Pip goes when I pop into the living room to ask if it's OK if I go round to Twig's for an hour. 'Are you going on a date?'

Mum looks up from the telly and smiles. She's

got a glass of wine – and has downed at least three sips – which is most prob why she says it's fine, as long as I'm back by half nine.

When I get round to Twig's, Sindi-Sue's there, helping Megan do a big clothes clear-out. It's really cool that they seem to have hit it off recently. Truth is, even though we've made up, I still find Megan a bit difficult to get on with sometimes. But I'm really glad that she and Sindi-Sue are getting to be mates – and she's definitely been acting less weird since we all started hanging out . . .

Twig and me are about to go out for a walk when Megan insists on dragging me upstairs to choose something from her cast-offs before she packs them up for the charity shop. It's obvious that Megan doesn't know yet about the Y-Generation disaster, so I don't mention it.

When I step through her bedroom door my heart double flips. Phoenix Macleod is staring at me from every wall! I'd totally forgotten how crazy Megan is about him. She's even got a huge poster on the ceiling above her bed.

'I go to sleep every night gazing into his eyes,' Megan giggles, and a little voice inside me whispers, *Actually, I don't blame you!* (Out of loyalty to Twig, I ignore it, of course.)

'Anyway, the reason I'm giving all this stuff to charity,' Megan continues as she tips one of her drawers out on to the bed, 'is cos I figure you and

Twig have the right attitude. You know, being green and everything. I got caught up in the whole buy-buy-buy thing. Like I thought it would make me happy, having tons of stuff, especially after Mum and Dad split up. But it doesn't help, not really . . .' She sighs heavily as she chucks a shimmery lemon sweatshirt on to her 'rejects' pile. 'In fact, Sindi-Sue and me were just saying it's like eating junk food. You eat and eat and eat and ten minutes later you're hungry again, and you can't work out why.'

'Yeah,' says Sindi-Sue, holding up a pair of orange leggings. 'I am so tired of my room being like TOTALLY clogged up with stuff. Sometimes I can hardly open the door. So once we've cleaned out Megan's, we're going round to do mine.'

Quickly – cos I really do want to be alone with Twig! – I settle on a lilac vest top. Then I hug Megan and Sindi-Sue and, relieved to get away from all those posters of Phoenix, I rush downstairs.

'I thought you'd still be wrecked from the Y-Generation thing,' Twig says as we wander aimlessly along the street.

'I was,' I explain, 'until Tas told me about the earthquake. That put it all in perspective. I realized it was totally silly getting so hung up on singing. There are tons of other things I can do.'

'But you're still gonna sing, surely?' Twig asks as we take the path that leads up to the swing park.

'Nope,' I reply, tossing my curls a bit, hoping he'll notice I've got mascara on. 'That's my past. I'd rather do something else now.'

'*What?* You're really going to give up singing, just cos Paradiso's are putting a block on you?' Twig exclaims, his eyes widening. 'That doesn't make sense, Sassy! Surely you should fight them, show them you can –'

'Look, I don't want to talk about it, OK?' I snap as I plonk on to a swing. Any thoughts I had of getting romantic have disappeared as fast as dirty dishwater down a plughole.

'So what do you want to talk about?' Twig shrugs. 'Global warming? The destruction of the rainforests? The melting ice caps? The droughts in Africa?'

I take a deep breath. 'Actually, I did see this programme on telly about how these lovely islands in the South Pacific are sinking into the sea,' My voice sounds lighter than my heart feels.

'Yeah, I saw that too,' Twig says, clambering up one of the swing support poles. 'Course they're not actually sinking; it's the level of the sea that's rising as the polar ice caps melt. Just like the world's top scientists have been predicting. The sea water's bubbling up through their farmland and the salt's killing their crops.'

He swings for a moment like a monkey, then jumps back to the ground.

'Look, I didn't mean to snap at you just then,' I say with a rueful smile.

'I know,' Twig looks at me through his flop of hair, and for a split second my heart does that fluttery thing and I think maybe, just maybe, he's gonna take my hands and pull me up off the swing and –

'I didn't take it personally,' Twig jumps on the swing next to me, then shouts, 'See who can go highest!' Next minute he's pushing off with his feet and swinging past me.

Honestly! I came out for a romantic reunion and Twig wants me to race him on the swings! Trying to hide my disappointment I watch as Twig sails higher and higher, hanging his head back so the wind rushes through his hair. And after a minute's sulking, I get a grip on myself. It looks like such fun, I think, so what the heck! Why not?

So I stand up on the seat and grab the chains and push off hard. Soon I catch up with him and for a few seconds we're swinging in perfect unison, the darkening sky rushing past above us, till finally we swing so high the chains lose their tension and clunk dangerously . . .

'OK, OK! I give in!' I scream.

Breathless, laughing, pink-cheeked, we let the swings slow to a gentle sway.

'I'd better get back home,' I say when I get my breath back. 'Mum will be wondering where I am.'

Wandering slowly across the park, it occurs to me how much I like Twig. How easy it is to be with him. We have so many things in common, like being passionate about the environment and wanting a fairer world and not liking uniforms and hating being ordered about by power-tripping adults, and all forms of violence.

But I can't help thinking that the more I get to know him, the more comfortable we get around each other, the less he seems like a boyfriend, the more he seems like a best bud. A very special best bud, but a best bud just the same.

I don't think that's how you're meant to feel about your boyfriend. Is it . . .?

11

It's Monday morning now and I can't say I'm looking forward to going into school.

I didn't see Cordelia over the weekend cos she was away with her mum at the Dark Arts Fair in Newcastle, but we had a long chat on the phone when she got back. At school on Friday she withheld the AWFUL TRUTH about Y-Generation pulling out of the record deal cos she thought I might want to keep it secret for a while. Instead she told everyone I was off with a tummy bug.

Eventually, of course, people will start to realize that my so-called singing career's going nowhere. But Cordelia figures that if it's a gradual process it will be easier for me to deal with. And I think she's right. I absolutely do not want to have a big dramatic meltdown in front of everyone at school.

As soon as I appear in Registration, Megan comes running over, wraps me in a bear hug in front of the whole class and wails, 'I am SO sorry you didn't get the record deal! Twig told me everything last night. You must be TOTALLY devastated. It's SO unfair!'

I stand there IN TOTAL SHOCK with everyone staring, like I'm the most pathetic, most-to-be-pitied creature on the planet!

When Megan releases me from her hug I make my way to my seat. People smile sadly. They murmur things like, 'Sorry Sass, better luck next time.' They throw me sympathetic looks like I've just been diagnosed with terminal diarrhoea. And I want to scream, *PLEASE STOP! I CAN'T HANDLE PITY! YOU'RE MAKING ME FEEL LIKE A VICTIM!!!*

But I don't. Cos it wouldn't be fair. No one means to be horrible to me. So instead I put on a professional smile, say 'No worries. I'm fine, actually.' And slide into my chair.

At last Miss Peabody comes in and takes the register and Sindi-Sue goes back to combing her hair; Karim Malik starts hiccupping cos he's accidentally swallowed a polo mint; Midge fools around trying to give him a fright to make him stop and Miss Peabody shouts *'Settle down, will you! This is a school, not a lunatic asylum!'* And for the first time ever I'm glad to sit really quietly with my head stuck in a book, not talking to anyone.

'You handled that really well,' Cordelia says as we trail along the corridor to the library. 'Megan shouldn't have put you in the spotlight like that.'

'Yeah,' I shrug. 'But that's Megan for you.'

'I wouldn't have blamed you if you'd blown up at her.' Cordelia adjusts the scarlet ribbons on her long black bunches.

'Well, I kinda wanted to. But like I said last night, I did a lot of thinking over the weekend. And I thought, actually, on the grand scale of things, not getting a recording deal isn't such a massive thing.[11] Not compared to an earthquake. So I made a decision. While I work out what I'm really gonna do with my life, I'm simply gonna be a better person and do five good deeds every day. I guess not blowing up at Megan was my first for today.'

Cordelia's face brightens. 'Hey! That's like that karma thing, isn't it?'

'Is it?' I ask as a posse of Fourth-Year boys push past, almost flattening us against the wall.

'Yeah. Karma. It's a Buddhist way of looking at life. If you do good things for other people, then good things will eventually come back to you. It might take a while. Like you might need to wait till your next life, you know, when you're reincarnated. As a donkey or a dolphin or something.'

'No chance of getting my karma a bit earlier? Like before I'm dead?' I ask as we wander into the

[11] I'm trying so hard, but the truth is it HURTS every time I think of it. *Sob sob.*

library and find a couple of quiet seats near the manga comic books.

'Sure,' Cordelia dumps her scary cat tote bag on the floor and smiles. 'That's the thing about karma. It works in a mysterious way. You have to do the right thing even if you think there's nothing in it for yourself.' She narrows her green eyes at me. 'And who knows, just when you don't expect it, you might get everything you ever hoped for.'

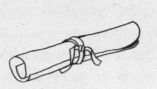

12

Phew! Cordelia got a text from Taslima last night. It simply said, *ARRIVED SAFELY*. But that's better than nothing, isn't it?

On the downside there were more reports from Pakistan on telly yesterday, and it's not looking good. Dad's newspaper this morning had a huge headline: *MORE DEVASTATION AS AFTER-SHOCKS CONTINUE*.

I had a quick read and Dad explained how after an earthquake, smaller earthquakes called after-shocks can continue for days and cause even more deaths and damage.

So Tas may have arrived safely, but we don't know how long ago her text was sent, and we don't actually know if she's still safe now.

We try texting back on Sindi-Sue's phone while we wait for Smollett to arrive for morning assembly. (Sindi-Sue's the only person with credit.) HOPE U R SAFE. MISSING YOU. LOL CORDELIA, SINDI-SUE, MEGAN & SASSY :o) xxx COME HOME SOON!

The text has just pinged off to Pakistan when Smollett sweeps on to the stage in his long black gown. He scowls until the hall falls silent. Then he cranks up his usual 'You-all-must-try-harder' motivational speech. Soon he's in full flow, waxing lyrical about lateness and poor attendance.

'Why's he going on at *us*?' Sindi-Sue whispers petulantly as she picks at the split ends in her hair. 'We're the ones who're here.'

'Yeah, *and* we've turned up on time,' Megan adds.

'Much more of this and next time I won't bother.' Cordelia mutters darkly.

As Smollett drones on, I zone out. Tas has a theory about school assemblies. She says they're nothing more than cheap therapy sessions for head teachers. Assemblies, according to Taslima, let them get things off their chests, and that stops them from having so many mental breakdowns.

'And now for some good news about a Strathcarron High student,' Smollett booms, and my brain zones back in. 'Magnus Menzies won three gold medals earlier this week at the Scottish Swimming Finals.' Smollett's face splits into a smile. 'I would like Magnus to come up on stage and collect a Student of Honour award.'

Grinning broadly, Magnus springs to his feet and bounces up the steps. A girl at the back of the hall wolf-whistles and Smollett's smile fades. Lovelace, the PE teacher, swoops and removes her with the swiftness and efficiency of a velociraptor.

Up on stage, Smollett beams as he hands Magnus a tube of rolled-up paper tied with a black ribbon. 'Keep up the good work, Magnus. You're a credit to the school. Thank goodness Strathcarron High has one star student.'

And that's when it happens. Someone shouts. 'What about Sassy Wilde?'

'Yeah,' another voice calls. 'Sassy Wilde's a star student. She was on telly!'

Smollett's face turns puce – well, his whole head, actually, cos he's bald as a coot[12] – and my heart thumps, cos if he calls me up on to the stage I'll have to tell THE WHOLE SCHOOL that I blew it, I'm not gonna be a star after all, I'm simply gonna be A Good Person – and something tells me that won't make me very popular.

Smollett bellows for silence and thankfully the hall immediately quietens. Then he starts reading out notices about library opening hours and stuff. And my heartbeat's just returning to normal when someone starts up – not much louder than a whisper – 'SASS-EE, SASS-EE, SASS-EE!' Suddenly, more people start going 'SASS-EE, SASS-EE, SASS-EE,' and others join in and the noise grows louder. **'SASS-EE, SASS-EE, SASS-EE!'**

---

[12] I have no idea what a coot is. Maybe coots go around saying, 'He's bald as a Smollett.' Who knows?

Smollett looks alarmed – but not half as alarmed as me!

Then as if by magic, the bell rings. Some chairs get knocked over and a book flies through the air. A few of the wilder kids make the most of the general commotion. Those who don't want to be part of a riot jump to their feet and head for the doors and the chanting fades as teachers round up what's left of their classes and hurry them to the exits.

'This is awful,' I groan as I stumble out between Megan and Cordelia. 'It's absolutely the last thing I needed. I mean everyone's gonna totally hate me when they find out I'm not gonna be a star.'

'They're not. Just keep a low profile,' Cordelia hisses in my ear. 'They'll soon forget.'

'Yeah, after a while they'll say things like, "Oh, remember how we all thought Sassy Wilde was gonna make it – but she never did,"' Megan adds as we hurry upstairs.

'Gee, thanks, Megan,' I mutter. 'That makes me feel a whole lot better.'

'Ah, Sassy Wilde, Superstar!' Miss Smith grins as we enter the IT lab. 'Mr Smollett just phoned. You've been summoned to his office. Right away.'

'He probably wants your autograph!' Midge Murphy quips as he hurtles around the room on a computer chair.

'More like he's going to lecture you on how you must take your schoolwork seriously.' Miss Smith tucks her latest romantic novel, *The Moon, the Man, His Mother and Me* into the top drawer of her desk.

'Yeah,' I mutter, chucking my bag down beside my chair. 'By pulling me out of class so I miss half the lesson. Very helpful I don't think.'

And with that I hurry from the room and head with a heavy heart towards Mr Smollett's office.

Miss Crump, the school secretary – a thin-lipped woman with hair like a sick coconut and dead-fish eyes – instructs me to sit on the row of chairs outside her glass window. Chairs normally reserved for kids who have done wrong, for kids who are in BIG TROUBLE, for kids who are ABOUT TO GET EXCLUDED.

Five minutes later, I'm still sitting there.

Fifteen minutes later, and, yes, sigh, I'm still there.

Obviously Mr Smollett, who according to the sign on his door is a Doctor of Science, has not quite grasped the concept of time. When Very Important People like Mr Smollett say *Right away*, what they really mean is *any time in the next millennium*.

I might grow old sitting here. Dust may settle on me. My bones might start to crumble. Archaeologists from the future may find my body . . .

Just last week I read about this woman who died after a flight from New York to London cos she'd had to sit still in the one place too long. She got deep vein thrombosis when her blood all got stuck in her feet. I wiggle each foot in turn to keep the blood flowing in my legs. I don't want to die, I'm too young to die –

'Mr Smollett is ready to see you now,' Miss Crump interrupts my thoughts. Relieved to still be alive I jump up. The seat makes a noise like a deflating balloon. Miss Crump eyes me suspiciously, like she thinks *I've* just made a rude noise. Which I certainly have not. There's enough pollution in the world from the digestive systems of cows and sheep without me adding to it, thank you.

As I enter his office, Smollett's standing behind his desk, and without even asking me to sit down he launches into a full lecture on how he doesn't care who my father is, there's absolutely no room for celebrities at Strathcarron High.

'No sweat, Sir,' I reply when he *eventually* lets me get a word in edgeways. 'I'm not going to be a celebrity anyway. That's all in the past. I am simply going to be a good person. So really, you have nothing to worry about.'

Then he gives me a punishment exercise for being cheeky!

Honestly, sometimes life is so unfair. So much for Cordelia's daft ideas about karma. Even when I'm trying my best to be good, I end up in trouble!

It's Wednesday lunchtime now and the Eco Club is meeting in Miss Cassidy's room. Cordelia and me get there first and organize some tables in a big square. Megan and Sindi-Sue have promised to come, but they're going to the lunch hall first to get sandwiches.

As Miss Cassidy takes out her lunchbox we try to peer discreetly in. Tas has a theory that you can work out the psychological profile of a person based on the contents of their lunch box. Midge Murphy, for example, always has a banana, which means he's . . . well . . . bananas. And Cordelia swears she knows for a fact that ancient, wrinkly little Miss Riley has a prune every day.

Cordelia stifles a giggle as Miss Cassidy takes out a small bag of nuts and pops one in her mouth. Then Sindi-Sue, Megan, Beano and Mad Midge arrive.

'OK,' I say, closing the door and returning to my seat. 'As Tas isn't here, Cordelia has agreed to be secretary.'

Cordelia opens our Eco Club folder and clears her throat. 'Right. So far we've convinced the head to buy energy-saving light bulbs; we've set up monitoring of the recycling bins for paper and aluminium cans; all school vegetable waste is now being composted, and we've got the school canteen and tuck shop to stock only Fair Trade produce –'

Just then the door crashes open. And – can you believe it? – in saunters Magnus Menzies! Honestly! That boy does not have an environmentally conscious bone in his body! How dare he turn up at Eco Club of all things!

But before I can suggest he leaves, Miss Cassidy only goes and shifts her seat over, pulls up an empty chair and says, 'There's room here, Magnus. Come and join us.'

Magnus gives me a big lovesick grin as he squeezes in beside her. It's enough to make me rush out into the corridor and throw up!

In the nick of time I remember my resolution to be nice. 'Welcome to Eco Club, Magnus.' The words almost stick in my throat. But hey-ho! I manage them. Just.

Miss Cassidy smiles. 'Yes, Magnus. Welcome on board.'

'Anything I can do to help the environment, Miss,' Magnus grins.

'So,' I say, pointedly blanking Magnus. 'Anyone got any idea what we should do next?'

'*I* do, actually,' Megan pipes up and we all look at her. 'Well, you know how there's tons of people affected by the earthquake . . . and . . . well, I think we should do something to raise money to help them. We can do other eco-stuff after the school hols, but people in the earthquake need help now.'

'Yeah, I'm all for that,' says Sindi-Sue, carefully peeling the skin from a grape. 'It would be good to think we were helping people somewhere else. We need to think global. And it would mean a lot to Tas when she gets back. Like a gesture of solidarity-type thing. And I mean, all these disasters, they're caused by global warming and stuff, so it's a good thing for Eco Club to do, right?'

'Not exactly,' Magnus chips in – and I try not to rankle. 'Earthquakes aren't actually caused by global warming, Sindi-Sue.'

'Whatever,' Sindi-Sue shrugs.

'But it's a good idea,' I say, eyeballing Magnus. 'And I think we should do it. We could raise money for tents and blankets and water purification tablets and all sorts of stuff.'

Everyone makes noises of agreement.

'So how do we raise the money?' Cordelia asks, tapping her pen against her teeth. 'Any ideas?'

Midge's hand shoots up. 'Yeah, me, I've got an idea!' We all stare, surprised. Midge is not known as an ideas person. 'We could hold a car wash,' he continues. 'You know, get the teachers to pay us to clean their cars.'

'That sounds so-o-o boring!' Megan complains, picking the cucumber from her salad and arranging it in a neat pile.

'Yeah, but I wasn't thinking of any old car wash!' Midge grins cheekily.

'So what kind of car wash do you have in mind?' Miss Cassidy asks.

'A *bikini* car wash!' he says triumphantly.

We look at him, confused.

'I saw one on telly. The girls – and you too if you want, Miss – wash the teachers' cars, you know, for a few quid each. And here's the really good bit. You all get to wear bikinis!' Midge puffs himself up. 'Of course, the men would fill the buckets.' He winks at Magnus. 'Do all the heavy work.'

Cordelia rolls her eyes. Megan stifles a giggle.

'Men?' says Sindi-Sue, coolly looking around the room. 'I don't see any men.'

Midge and Magnus bristle.

'I don't think so, Midge,' Miss Cassidy says quickly. 'Anyway, it's probably better to do something simple and easy that doesn't take too much organizing. Then you can send off some money to the earthquake fund almost immediately.'

'I've got it!' Megan blurts excitedly. 'We go to Paradiso's after school – it's always really busy there – and we have buckets with *EARTHQUAKE*

DISASTER FUND written on. Then we ask people as they come out to give us their loose change.'

'Yeah,' says Sindi-Sue excitedly. 'The Boys' Brigade or Scouts or whatever those dudes in uniform are, well, they were doing that at the checkouts last week. I saw people putting pound coins in. I bet they made tons.'

'I'm up for it,' says Magnus – grinning at me again like a lovesick dolphin.

'Me too,' Megan giggles.

'OK,' I say. 'It looks like we're decided. So when will we do it?'

'Why not today?' Cordelia looks round at everyone. 'We can meet at Paradiso's at what, half past four?'

Then the bell goes and we all hurriedly stuff our wrappers in the bin and put the tables back where they were. As we file into the corridor, I swear Magnus goes out of his way to bump into me.

I take a deep breath and pull him to one side. 'Listen, Magnus,' I say quietly. 'You may as well know. I'm not going to be a star. Ever. I've given up singing. So you can stop trying to get together with me. OK?'

Magnus gives me a hurt look. 'How shallow do you think I am?'

And before I can think of an answer, he goes jogging off down the corridor.

14

After school I head straight home. And I'm about to grab some munchies when my mobile pings. I dig it out of the bottom of my bag, hoping it's a text from Taslima. But it's not. It's from Twig: Gone to Mums for fw days. C U when I get back.

I stare at the screen. I mean, if he was a real boyfriend wouldn't he have put at least ONE tinsy little kiss?

I'm pouring a glass of juice and feeling totally discombobulated and wishing Tas was around to give me some advice on what to do about Twig – when my mobile pings again. For a daft moment I think Twig's maybe sent me a separate text with the missing kiss, or maybe even one saying something like: Actually I'm really gonna miss U. U R most beautiful girl on planet. Can't wait 2 C U when I get bak. LOL, TWIG xxxxxxxxx

I glance at the screen. And it *is* a sweet text.

A really sweet text. But it's not from Twig. It's from Phoenix. `Hi Sassy! How R things? Hope U R not too down. Keep singing Crazy Girl! U R very special. Speak soon. LOL Phoenix x`

Troubled, I stare at Phoenix's message. To be honest, it's more like a text from a boyfriend than the one I got from Twig. Phoenix has even put a kiss. And what does he mean by *LOL*? *Laugh Out Loud*, or *Lots of Love*? And if he means *Lots of Love*, does that mean something or not?

Confused, I'm about to shove my mobile in my pocket when it occurs to me I'd better text Phoenix back – in case he thinks I'm not speaking to him. Something innocent, though – I mean, I still have a boyfriend . . . don't I? Finally I decide on: `Hi Phoenix! Thnx 4 all texts. Am good. Sassy x`

Just then Brewster wakes, stretches and sticks his nose in his empty bowl. Now *dogs* I understand. Grateful for the distraction, I fetch a can of dog food. Brewster smiles up at me and wags his tail joyfully. Dogs are so much more straightforward than boys! I open the can and give him some disgusting-smelling meat (which I hope hasn't got dolphins or horses or whales or anything like that in) and a fresh bowl of water.

Then I shove all thoughts of boys to the back of my mind cos I'm supposed to be meeting up with Cordelia and Megan in ten minutes. Two-at-a-time

I run upstairs and change into my Friends of the Fowl Tee – you know, the one with the big yellow chicken on the front – and a pair of old jeans. Then I leap downstairs (two-at-a-time) and tug Mum's mop bucket out of the kitchen cupboard.

I scream with frustration as hundreds of plastic bags and a box crammed with rags and dusters all fall out as well. When I try to stuff them back in, the ironing board tips forward and clobbers me on the head. Honestly, this house is a death trap! I don't know how me and Pip have survived. A few years ago, when she was teensy, Pip opened the airing-cupboard door and Mum's ironing pile avalanched. I had to use Brewster as a sniffer dog. It took us two hours to find her.

I make a mental note to tell my mother that for Health and Safety reasons she should keep her cupboards better organized, then I stuff the ironing board and all the rest of the junk back in. The door won't close quite right so I have to give it an almighty heave with my bottom. By which point I'm all hot and bothered. But, I remind myself as I pick up the bright red mop bucket and head out, not as hot and bothered as I would be if I was slap-bang in the middle of an earthquake.

First stop is Cordelia's. Did I mention that Cordelia's house is above her mum's shop, The Magic Broomstick? It's one of the oldest buildings in Strathcarron and it sells all sorts of witchy stuff, like candles and crystals and tarot cards – oh, and clothes too. If you want anything weird in black or purple, or you want to set up your own altar to Wicca, then The Magic Broomstick's your kinda place.

Cordelia's mum is busy reading a customer's palm when I go in. As I slip through the long beaded curtain to go through to the house behind the shop, a cacophony of tiny bells tinkles mystically and it's as if I'm entering a magical world.

Cordelia and Megan are at the big table in the kitchen, with paper and coloured pens scattered everywhere, making signs to stick on the collection buckets.

EARTHQUAKE DISASTER FUND
PLEASE GIVE GENEROUSLY

Cordelia's doing the printing with a fat black marker pen, and Megan's adding little red crosses.

'I'm a bit worried that we're not going to be very eye-catching. People are always in a hurry when they're shopping. Maybe we should make something to draw attention to ourselves? Like a big banner or something.' Cordelia says thoughtfully.

'Yeah,' Megan says excitedly, 'sometimes people collecting for charity wear fancy dress –'

'Well, we can hardly wear fancy dress!' I exclaim

as I try to tape a label to my bucket. 'I mean, people in the earthquake zone are injured and dying. It would be a bit off to, like, dress up as a clown or a teddy bear, to collect money for a disaster.'

'I've got it!' Cordelia leaps up from her chair. 'You're brilliant, Sassy! Of course! It's so obvious!'

'Sorry,' I ask, confused. 'What's so obvious?'

'One of us should dress up as an earthquake victim! You know, with, say, a bandage round the head, an arm in a sling, that sort of thing. People could hardly just walk by and ignore us, could they?'

'Isn't that a bit . . . errr . . . sick?' Megan looks doubtful.

'Yeah, but it would make people stop and think,' I say. 'You know, about how lucky they are and how awful it would be if our streets were filled with hurt and dying people.'

'And it's not like we're doing it to keep the money for ourselves,' Cordelia chips in. 'So I think it's a good idea.'

'Well, don't blame me if it all goes wrong,' Megan says with a sigh. 'And don't expect me to be the one who gets dressed up, either.'

'No probs,' I exclaim. 'I'm happy to be the victim. But where will we get the bandages and stuff?'

'Leave that to me!' Cordelia heads for the door. 'I've got tons of bandages and things in my Dolls' Hospital –'

Megan and I burst out laughing.

'I don't still play with it!' Cordelia adds quickly as she disappears upstairs.

'Don't worry,' I call after her. 'Your secret's safe with us.'

There's a clattering from the floor above as Cordelia rummages under her bed. Moments later she returns lugging a small suitcase with a wobbly red cross painted on. She hoists it on to the table, clicks the catches and lifts the lid. Inside lie a tangle of bandages, brown medicine bottles, play syringes – and a huge pile of dismembered dolly arms and legs and decapitated heads!

'Spare parts,' Cordelia says quickly as she lays the dolly bits to one side. 'I liked playing at surgeons when I was little. Unfortunately some of my . . . err . . . patients, didn't quite survive.'

I volunteer to be the earthquake victim. Megan wraps a bandage round my head while Cordelia bandages up my leg. Then Megan finds a triangular bandage for an arm sling and Cordelia rushes off to the garden shed and comes back with an ancient pair of cobweb-covered crutches her mum once had when she broke her ankle. In no time at all I'm transformed from a healthy, happy-go-lucky schoolgirl, into a one-person-disaster-area.

Cordelia and Megan stand back to admire their handiwork.

'Just two more things,' Cordelia says and rushes

out to the back garden again, this time reappearing with a small plant pot full of earth.

'Here, smear this over your face a bit,' she instructs. Then she disappears through to her mum's shop. Moments later she comes back with four or five dark red phials. 'Fake blood!' she cackles, as she squirts it at my bandages.

'Right. That's you all ready now,' Cordelia says at last. 'Take a look in the mirror up in my room.'

With some difficulty – my left leg is so tightly bandaged I can hardly move it – I hobble upstairs and into Cordelia's room. I almost faint when I see my reflection. What a mess!

'Brilliant!' I say as I hobble back into the kitchen. 'If nothing else this should put Magnus Menzies right off me!'

'Sindi-Sue just texted.' Megan picks up a couple of buckets. 'She'll be outside Paradiso's in ten minutes.'

'And so will we,' I grin, leaning heavily on my crutches. 'Let's go! We're bound to get lots of people to give to us now!'

Paradiso's is mobbed with tons of mums dragging tired, hungry kids around after them. We meet up with Magnus, Midge, Beano and Sindi-Sue by the trolley park and plan our strategy.

The best time to catch people, Magnus figures, is *after* they've done their shopping, when they return to their cars in the car park. 'Nobody wants to be bothered on the way in,' he reasons, cos they just want to get their shopping over and done with. But if we catch them as they get back to their cars, the kids have usually been bought off with sweets or crisps, and cos they're all heading home they're in a better mood.'

I think about arguing with Magnus, just for the sake of it. Then I remember my resolution to be a better person, so I button it.

'OK!' Cordelia picks up her bucket, 'Let's get started.' She spots a woman with a trolley piled high with shopping and a little kid trailing after her. We watch admiringly as Cordelia catches up with them just as they reach a four-wheel drive.

'Earthquake Disaster Fund. Please give generously,' Cordelia smiles, pushing her bucket under the woman's nose.

The kid stares up at Cordelia. 'You're freaky!' he giggles.

'Into the car, Felix!' the woman snaps as she dumps her shopping in the boot. 'And how many times do I have to tell you not to speak to strangers!' Then she gets in and revs her engine and roars off, almost running over Cordelia's toes.

Cordelia shrugs and heads towards a man in a business suit who's just opening the door of his sports car. With a charming smile she pushes her bucket towards him.

'Sorry, love,' he says, shaking his head. 'I only carry plastic. Not got a penny on me.'

The rest of us don't do much better. I hobble over to a fat baldy man with tattoos and shake my bucket under his nose. 'Earthquake in Pakistan,' I say sweetly. 'Please give generously.'

'And what's anyone from Pakistan ever done to help me?' he scowls.

'I don't want to be rude,' I splutter. 'But personally I don't think you should have to check what nationality someone is before you decide whether or not to help them!' I turn on my heel and hobble off.

'It's not going to be quite as easy as we thought,' Cordelia sighs as she comes back over to where Magnus, Sindi-Sue, Beano, Megan and me are once more huddled in a group. 'When people are near their cars it's too easy for them to get in and drive away.'

'I think we should try right outside the main doors,' Megan says. 'People sometimes still have their purses in their hands as they come out, so it's not so hard for them to cough up some change.'

'Yeah,' says Magnus. 'And Sassy should be more . . . more . . . visible. Like more upfront. More dramatic. I mean, maybe you could lie on the ground and kind of pretend like you're really injured.'

'Yeah, like you on the football field!' The words slip out before I can stop them.

'Exactly!' Magnus laughs. 'I'm sure a great performer like you can manage that.'

So we all head over to the sliding exit doors. It's true there are tons more people there. In fact the whole place is even busier now than when we first arrived. So I take up a position on the paving slabs and lie down, writhing and moaning while the others circulate with their buckets.

'This is great!' Megan grins after five minutes. 'Look, I've got three quid already!' She rattles her bucket and two little girls come skipping over and drop a scattering of silver coins in.

So I step up my performance a bit, moaning and holding my hands out like I've seen victims do in films. And it's all going really well, when a big pair of black boots appears beside my face. I look up. Above the black boots are black trousers; above the black trousers, a black jerkin. I pull myself up to a sitting position. A big red face scowls down at me. Oh no! It's a Paradiso's security guard!

'And what exactly do you think you're doing, young lady?' he asks. Which really annoys me. I mean, why do grown-ups always address you in an over-polite way when they quite clearly are not actually being polite at all?

'Isn't it kind of obvious?' I look around desperately for Cordelia and the others, who seem to have suddenly vanished.

He purses his lips and shakes his head slowly.

'I'm injured,' I say, with what I hope is a winning smile. 'Quite badly, actually. You know, broken leg, dislocated shoulder, massive internal injuries. That's why I'm lying on the ground. I've been in an earthquake.'

'And which earthquake would that be?' the guard asks drily. 'Can't say I noticed it.' He chortles at his own wit.

'The one in North Pakistan,' I reply.

By this point a small crowd of shoppers has gathered round. I have a horrible flashback to the last run-in I had with a Paradiso's security guard. But, I remind myself, it was *Mum* who got us into hot water that time. *I* wasn't to blame. And *that* security guard was called Bill. *This* one – I strain to see his name badge – is Bob.

Bob stops pursing his lips and smiles, and I'm thinking, gosh, wonders will never cease – a Paradiso's security guard with a social conscience!

I reach for my collection bucket and push it towards him. 'Would you like to give?' I say hopefully. 'Generously?'

'I think you'll find, young lady,' he says, his smile fading, 'that the Pakistani earthquake affected a five-hundred-mile radius. And unless I'm much mistaken, Scotland escaped unscathed.'

Just then three things happen.

One: another security guard comes striding out of the store.

Two – and this is the bad bit: I recognize him. It's Bill.

Three – and this is the REALLY bad bit: Bill recognizes me, his face darkens and his mouth sets itself in a hard line.

'YOU!' he exclaims. 'Not blind any more, I see. Oh, and crutches this time! Pretending to be disabled, are we?'

'But . . .' I begin, looking around desperately for my so-called friends to back me up. 'It's not the way it looks . . . You don't understand . . .'

Bill hauls me roughly to my feet. 'I understand only too well. You types! I suppose your mother's lurking somewhere in your rickety van, waiting for you to get back with a bucketload of cash, eh?' He scans the car park. 'Looks like she's deserted you this time! I think you'd better come with me, young lady.'

And before I can object, he bundles me into the store and towards a door marked *SECURITY*.

The next ten minutes are like something from a nightmare – the kind you try to wake up from but can't. Bill shoves me on to a chair and glowers fiercely at me.

'Maybe her mum felt a bit hard up,' Bill says sarcastically. 'So she thought up a neat wheeze. Dress the kid up as an earthquake victim. Get good, kind people to cough up their hard-earned dosh. Then skedaddle off to the shops on a spending spree.'

I open my mouth to protest, then close it again. They've not believed anything I've told them so far, so why would I expect them to start listening now? And I can't tell them who I REALLY am, can I? I mean, how's it going to look when they find out my dad's the local MP?

Bob makes a quick phone call. Within minutes two policemen appear.

'Trying to get money by extortion is a very serious business,' the taller policeman says as he inspects the bucket with its handmade sign. 'Let's see. You don't have a licence to collect. You don't have permission from Paradiso's to be on their property. And you're not connected to any official charity. So what do you have to say for yourself?'

'I refuse to say anything till I've spoken to my lawyer,' I say desperately, cos I remember hearing something like that in a film once. 'I want to exercise my right to silence. I invoke the Fourth Amendment.'

The police officers roll their eyes. Bill and Bob laugh heartily. 'This isn't some cop film,' Bill says.

'Tell you what,' the tall police officer says when they all stop chuckling. 'We'll take this young lady home. Have a word with her parents. See if they can get some control over her.'

'Met the mother before, mate,' Bill snorts. 'One of those new-age hippy types. Bring the kids up with no morals at all, that lot do. Stealing's just a way of life for them.'

Minutes later I'm being led out of a side door of the store. I think of making a run for it. I desperately do NOT want them to find out who I really am. But I'm hardly going to be able to outrun two cops with my leg bandaged up so tight I can't bend it, one arm in a sling and crutches, am I?

As I get into the panda car I consider my options:

1. Pretend I have sudden amnesia and can't remember who I am or where I live
2. Lie about who I am, give a false address and tell them they'd best not come into the house cos my mum has the Black Death and it's highly infectious
3. Tell the truth. Hope that they're impressed that my dad's a lawyer and the local MP, and that Mum then wins them over with a nice cup of tea and some lovely home-made muffins.

As the tall police officer starts the engine, he looks over his shoulder to where I'm sitting in the back.

'OK, love,' he says. 'Where to?'

15

Whoop! For once it's all worked out OK. Who knows, maybe at last my luck is changing and I'm starting to get some of that GOOD karma Cordelia was talking about . . .

In the end I give the police my proper name and address and, of course, they know who Dad is. And it turns out the tall policeman's big sister was best friends with my mum at school and he immediately says, 'What on earth was that security guard going on about? Heather's not a new-age hippy!' And I explain that they were really rude and horrible to Mum before and I tell them all about Taslima and the earthquake and how me and my friends were only trying to raise money to help and they say, 'Oh, that all makes sense now!'

So when we get home they come in with me and the tall policeman explains how there's been a bit of a misunderstanding at Paradiso's and the security guards have been unnecessarily heavy-handed – and guess what? Mum takes MY side totally and is railing on about phoning Paradiso's up and complaining, but instead she gets sidetracked making tea for the two policemen and serving them some totally mouth-watering lemon drizzle cake, and the policemen tell Mum about me demanding my right to silence under the Fourth Amendment and now they're all hooting with laughter.

'So what's wrong with that?' I ask, my colour rising. 'I thought that was what you were supposed to say.'

'Well, first of all,' Mum grins, 'it's the *Fifth* Amendment.'

'And second,' the tall policeman splutters through a mouthful of lemon drizzle cake, 'that's only in America!'

I leave them to their laughter and hobble upstairs. Actually I don't mind them laughing at me. For a while back there I thought Dad would be grounding me, like, forever, for dragging his name into disrepute by getting arrested and brought home in a police car like a common criminal.

Now all I want to do is get out of my bandages and cleaned up – and find out what happened to Cordelia and Megan and everyone else. I mean, so OK, I didn't get flung in jail, but I can't imagine it's been Mission Successful. As far as I know the buckets were pretty empty when the security guards busted us.

I limp into the bathroom, close the door, pull off

all my bandages and filthy clothes and have a quick shower. Then I wrap myself in a big bath towel and whizz downstairs to grab the cordless phone from the hall table before anyone sees me wandering around half naked. Then I bound back upstairs two-at-a-time.

But as I open the door to my bedroom I get such a shock I almost drop the phone – and the towel!

'Shhhhh . . .' Cordelia says, leaping at me and clamping her hand over my mouth. 'No one knows we're here! We didn't want to shop you to your mum. So we came in through the window.' (*We?!*)

I do a double take – and grip the towel extra-super-tight. Everyone from Eco Club's in my room! Sindi-Sue and Megan flutter their fingers at me.

Magnus grins. 'Hi! Love the towel.'

Midge ogles.

I blush from the end of my little toe right up my legs, right to the tips of my ears. 'Er – give me a minute,' I squeak, rushing quick as a flash back through to the bathroom and slamming the door shut . . . only to realize I've no clothes with me! I stare unhappily at the filthy ones I've just taken off, lying in a pathetic heap on the floor. Then I scan the pile of towels in the cupboard, wondering desperately if I can wear them like a kind of burkha to stop Midge ogling me while I grab some clothes from my room.

I'm searching for the hugest bath towel when

there's a tap at the door. 'It's me!' says Cordelia. 'Thought you might need some clothes.'

More than a little relieved, I open the door and grab the shorts and Tee Cordelia shoves at me.

'See,' Cordelia grins before heading back into my room. 'Sometimes it's useful to have a friend who's psychic!'

Ten minutes later I am fully dressed, my decency and modesty intact.

'So what happened to you at Paradiso's?' Megan asks as I collapse on to my beanbag. 'Tell us everything!'

'What happened to *me*? What happened to you lot, more like? One minute you were all there; next thing it was just me and the security guard.'

'Sorry about that,' Cordelia sighs. 'We saw him coming and tried to warn you –'

'– but you were so caught up in all your writhing and moaning,' Megan continues, 'we couldn't get your attention.'

'So we legged it round the side of the building and hid, you know, to wait. But you never came back out, so in the end we decided to head back here.' Cordelia finishes.

They listen in shocked silence as I tell them all about my trauma with the security guards and the police.

'You poor thing!' Megan gasps.

'Oh, it's nothing,' I say bravely. 'And at least it all turned out OK when I got home.'

Then Cordelia suggests we count what we've collected and Magnus climbs back down to the garden to get the buckets. We tip the takings out on to the centre of my rainbow rug and Magnus and Megan put the coins into little piles.

'OK,' Magnus says at last. 'Seven pounds, thirty-two pence, one euro, two buttons and, oh, a pink Love Heart that says,' he glances up at me, '*Darling, be mine.*'

I scowl to warn him off. And guess what? He only turns and offers it to Megan! Course, I'm expecting her to throw it back in his face on account of what happened at her party that time – but she turns more pink than the Love Heart, simpers, 'Thanks, Magnus. I'll think about it,' and pockets it!

Cordelia and me exchange a what's-going-on-there? look.[13]

'I had hoped we'd get a lot more than a measly seven quid,' I mutter. 'I mean, that's hardly going to make a difference when whole towns have been reduced to rubble.'

We stare dejectedly at the little pile.

'Well,' Cordelia says slowly, 'there's only one thing for it, then.' We all look at her as if we

[13] Wide eyes, raised eyebrows, puckered lips.

expect her to cast a magic spell over the money and turn it into twenty-pound notes, like that Rumpelstiltskin dude when he turned the straw into gold for what's-her-name locked in the tower by the evil king.

'Oh, it's nothing magic!' she says quickly as if she's read our minds[14]. 'Much more down to earth than that. And it will involve all of us mucking in and doing a fair bit of work –'

'Well, I'm up for it,' Magnus says immediately.

'Me too,' says Megan as Sindi-Sue nods in agreement. 'It would be great to be able to tell Taslima when she comes back that we raised, like, a hundred pounds for the disaster fund.'

'And I don't mind a bit of hard work!' I exclaim. 'Anything would be easy compared to getting taken prisoner by Paradiso's security guards and arrested by the police.'

Cordelia eyeballs me – which is a pretty scary experience. 'Are you sure about that, Sass?'

'Course I am,' I say forcefully. 'I want to do my best for Taslima. Course I do.'

'Omigod, Cordelia!' Megan gasps. 'You're not thinking about that stupid bikini car wash idea, are you? Cos if it's that, then you can COUNT ME OUT!'

'No way!' Cordelia laughs and shakes her head

[14] Which she probably has!

103

so her long black bunches swish softly. '*And* I think we can make more than a hundred pounds. Maybe even two hundred.' Her green eyes glitter.

'Well, I say we do it!' I say enthusiastically. 'Whatever it is!'

'So come on, Cordelia,' Magnus urges. 'What's the big idea?'

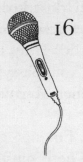

16

'No way! Absolutely not!' I exclaim.

'But you said you'd do *anything*!' Cordelia protests.

'Yeah, anything except *that*!' I pick up Tiny Ted and fire him at the mini-basketball ring on the back of my door. He misses totally and thwacks violently off the wall.

'But think about it,' Cordelia pleads. 'If you do a lunchtime concert at school we're bound to get *at least* a hundred kids in. You heard them at assembly. They WANT you to sing!'

'And if we charge them even just one pound each, well, that'd be a hundred pounds straight off,' Megan says excitedly.

'I think it's a brilliant idea!' Magnus grins.

'Well, that's cos it's not *you* who's got to get up on stage!' I protest.

'But I thought you LOVED getting up on stage.' Confusion flickers across Sindi-Sue's face.

'Not any more,' I say vehemently. 'Look, I'm not going to sing again ever. I've made my mind up –'

'But it's for a good cause!' Sindi-Sue protests. 'I mean, if *I* could sing, *I'd* do it, but let's face it,' she smiles ruefully, 'I don't think anyone would pay to hear me.'[15]

'So it's GOT to be you, Sassy!' Cordelia says simply. 'Or it can't happen. And we don't raise the money.'

'Look,' I splutter, 'I'm not going to do it. So forget about it. There must be something else . . .'

'Something that would raise over a hundred quid in one go?' Magnus shakes his head slowly. 'I don't think so.'

'Well, if there is, Sass, then you come up with it,' Cordelia eyeballs me again.

I think frantically. 'Er . . . Magnus could do a sponsored swim?'

'Obviously I could do a swim. Like, if anyone wants me to,' Magnus puffs himself up.

'That is SO-O-O-O boring,' Sindi-Sue exclaims. Then hurriedly adds with a quick flutter of her fingers at Magnus, 'No offence, Magnus, sweetie, but I just can't see people rushing to sponsor you. Anyway, sponsoring is really overdone, don't you think? And it's for little kids. I mean, we'll get much more money if we offer people something they can actually enjoy.'

[15] It's true. Sindi-Sue's karaoke is to die for – literally.

'Come on, Sassy,' Beano says with big pleading eyes. 'Think of how dull our sad little lives are. Our very own concert in Strathcarron would be ace!'

Everyone's staring at me now. And I feel awful. Cos deep down I know they're right. It probably *is* the easiest way to get a lot of money in a short time.

'I bet we could get old Smollett to give us the school hall for free,' Magnus suggests, like he's not understood that I'm not going to do it.

'And Miss Cassidy would let us make posters and stuff in her room,' Megan adds.

'And Beethoven would let us use the music studio equipment, you know, the amplifiers and stuff,' Sindi-Sue says excitedly. ('Beethoven' is actually Mr Beaton, our music teacher.)

'Look!' I interrupt. 'Stop making plans for something that is JUST NOT GOING TO HAPPEN!'

I feel so frustrated I want to stomp off to my room. But I'm in it already. 'And in any case,' I add more quietly. 'I CAN'T do it.'

'Why not?' Cordelia asks.

'Cos,' I say huffily.

'Cos what?' Cordelia persists, her green eyes narrowing.

I take a deep breath, then exhale slowly. 'Cos . . . I don't have a guitar. Not any more.'

'You don't have a guitar?' Megan gasps, looking

around, like she expects to see it propped against my desk where it used to sit. 'What do you mean?'

'I mean . . . that I gave it away. Last Friday. To the Oxfam shop.'

There's a shocked silence.

'I told you. I'm serious. I'm NOT going to sing again.' There's a quiver in my voice and I hate myself for not being able to control it. Tears brim in my eyes and I bite my bottom lip to stop them spilling over. My friends look embarrassed.

Suddenly, Magnus gets to his feet and clears his throat. 'Look, I think I'd better get going,' he says, then he climbs out the window on to the big branch of the tree and disappears through the leaves. Beano and Midge follow him.

'Is it OK if me and Megan use the door?' Sindi-Sue asks, standing up and tugging down her tiny denim skirt.

I nod.

'Don't worry,' Megan gives me a sad smile. 'OK, so seven quid's not much. But at least we raised something. At least we tried.'

I bite my lip hard to stop the tears spilling over. Grrrr . . . There's nothing worse for getting me all emotional than people showing me sympathy.

'See you tomorrow,' Cordelia says, giving me a quick hug.

As the door closes behind them I throw myself on to the bed and lie staring up at the ceiling.

All I want to do is forget that I could ever sing. To leave the old Sassy behind. Find someone new that I can be. I thought if I gave my guitar away that would be it. That I wouldn't ever have to think about singing again.

But it doesn't look like it's going to work out that way . . .

17

That night after tea I'm sitting in the front of the car with Digby, on the way to Fossil Grove Old Folks' Home. Dad's in the back working his way through a pile of constituency mail, which means Digby and I can't natter. Bored, I take out my mobile and flick through my saved messages. Four from Phoenix. One from Twig.

Deep in thought, I stare at the passing cars and houses. It's a warm evening and people are out cutting their lawns, unpacking shopping, chatting to their neighbours. Kids are playing in gardens. Everyone's life seems settled and ordered – except mine.

Just then Digby swings the car into a leafy drive and I tuck my mobile back into my pocket. *Fossil Grove, A Modern Residential Home For The Elderly* says a big sign. Seconds later, Digby pulls the car to a halt in a small car park. I get out and survey the building. It certainly looks state-of-the-art from the outside, with lots of glass. It's even got its own garden and big mature trees. It might well be the perfect place to stick Mum and Dad in a few years, you know, when they get gaga and can't look after themselves properly any more. I make a mental note to pay extra special attention to what it's got to offer. Hopefully I can help Dad make a good impression on the matron. I might even ask if there's a waiting list I can put the parentals' names on.

As we approach the entrance, Dad straightens his tie and puts his *I'm-an-MP* face on. Digby rings the buzzer. There's an old lady on the other side of the glass door staring at us like she thinks we're strange creatures from another planet. I smile and give a little wave, and while I wonder whether or not that's enough to count as a good deed, the sweet old lady raises one hand from her walking frame and waggles her bony fingers back at me.

Suddenly, the door swing opens and Dad and Digby step forward – but not before the sweet old lady seizes her chance and hurtles towards the open door as fast as an Olympic sprinter off the blocks!

Skilful as a slalom skier she weaves past Dad and Digby – just as two nurses appear from nowhere shouting, 'Stop her!'

I open my arms – and she knocks me over like a skittle. Honestly, she looks so frail, but I swear it was like getting hit by Brickhouse Britney from the Fifth Year in a rugby tackle. Of course, I cushion her fall, which is just as well, cos you hear all these stories about little old ladies and broken hips and how hard it is for them to mend.

While I gasp for breath the nurses pull her off and bundle her back into the home. I struggle to my feet, protesting that I'm fine, honestly. Not that anyone seems to care! Then I stagger through the glass doors while a nurse guards them till they close automatically behind me. Safely inside, I'm shocked when I see my reflection in a mirror. My T-shirt's all dusty from the path and I've got some dead leaves and twigs in my hair.

Before I can do anything to clean myself up, a middle-aged woman with a perfect dress and a perfect smile and perfect hair appears in front of us.

'Welcome to Fossil Grove,' she beams. 'I'm the matron, Mrs Pratchett. The residents are very excited about your visit.'

Mrs Pratchett gives us a tour of the home.

'It's lovely to see a young person taking an interest,' she beams as she shows me the delights of their disabled toilet facilities. I ask if I can possibly use the loo just to tidy myself up a bit, so she leaves me to it.

To be honest I find the disabled toilet a bit freaky. There are extra handles all over the place in case you're a bit unsteady on your feet, and as well as a mirror at normal eye height, there's a mirror at, well, bottom height, which gives me a kind of unfortunate view of myself when I sit down.

I wash my hands with the *Taps especially designed for the weaker grip of the elderly* as the label above them says, and I can't help but think that the old dear who careered into me at the front door is more than capable of using a normal tap, thank you. I dry my hands on the super fast hand-dryer, which is so strong I'm surprised a few little old ladies haven't been blown into orbit[16], then I prepare to rejoin Dad and Digby.

But no sooner have I stepped out of the loo than this deafening siren goes off and a red light above the door starts flashing. It's like something from a James Bond film where the superspy hits a trip wire and all the doors lock shut and baddies come flying from everywhere at once.

Automatically, I freeze and put my hands up. The little old lady who flattened me at the front door leans on her walking frame, smirking, as a male nurse pushes me aside, opens the toilet door behind me and pulls the red light cord. With a final thin wail the siren stops.

'The red one's the emergency cord,' the nurse says sternly. 'The white one puts the light out.' I glance into the toilet, reach past him and pull the white cord. The light goes out.

'Thanks,' I say sheepishly. 'I won't get it wrong again.'

[16] Or maybe they have. Must check the night sky tonight!

Digby and Dad stand staring at me. I can read the look on Dad's face. I have seen it many times before.

'Don't worry, Dad,' I whisper reassuringly as we follow Mrs Pratchett along a carpeted corridor where old people are dotted about like potted plants. 'I won't get anything else wrong. I promise.'

Quietly I follow Mrs Pratchett into the Sunset Rest Room. There are old people dozing here and there in high-backed armchairs, or sitting chomping their gums and dribbling, or spouting rubbish at anyone who'll listen. It reminds me of somewhere else, but it takes a few minutes before I place it.

Of course! It's just like the staffroom at Strathcarron High. I have a little giggle to myself as Dad and Digby chat to residents, most of whom seem to be hard of hearing.

'TURN YOUR HEARING AID ON, MR SMITH!' Mrs Pratchett bellows at an old man in a button-up cardigan. He fumbles for a minute in the pocket of his trousers, then pulls out a pair of specs and shakily shoves them on his nose.

'YOUR HEARING AID!' Mrs Pratchett attempts again, and several old dears who had been dozing, their mouths hanging open, are startled awake.

Next Mrs Pratchett ushers us through to the Sunshine Activity Room. I heave a sigh of relief.

The old people in here show signs of life. Some of the women are knitting and chattering. Others are playing cards and dominoes. There's even an elderly couple playing table tennis. And they're pretty good.

A murmur of excitement runs around the room as Mrs Pratchett calls for silence.

'Ladies and gentlemen,' she announces with a very pleased look. 'Our Very Important Visitor is here. I have great pleasure in presenting to you our new Member of Parliament, Mr Angus Wilde and his assistant, Digby.' Mrs Pratchett doesn't introduce me. Obviously she's one of those annoying grown-ups who think teenagers don't count as people.

Dad preens himself, clears his throat and launches into a speech all about how important the 'silver' vote is and how he and his party will have the concerns of old people at the top of their political agenda.

'After all,' Dad says grandly – and he pauses for effect – 'if a society doesn't look after its elderly, what does that say about it?'

There's a polite ripple of applause. Mrs Pratchett looks pleased. 'And now Mr Wilde has very kindly agreed to answer any questions you may have for him.'

There's a silence. Then suddenly, a man with a mop of silver hair and gold-rimmed specs sticks his hand up. Mrs Pratchett nods at him like an infant teacher giving a child permission to speak.

'It's a question for the kid,' the silver-haired man says gruffly. Mrs Pratchett raises an eyebrow, Dad's face falls and a strange mix of disappointment and apprehension flits across it. I throw him a *don't-worry-Dad-I'll-handle-it* look. The silver-haired man takes his glasses off and squints at me like he's trying to focus, then his face lights up.

'I knew it!' he says triumphantly. 'I never forget a face. You were on telly! Singing at that festival. That was you, wasn't it?'

Dad's face is a perfect picture of panic. Deep inside I feel a small sharp pain, cos I have consigned anything to do with my past life to the trash can of my heart. But I keep my cool.

'Yes,' I say, trying to sound like it's no big deal. 'That was me.'

'Now,' Mrs Pratchett interrupts, a note of impatience creeping in at the edge of her voice. 'I know some of you have questions for Mr Wilde –'

'We thought you were very good,' a woman with bouncy white curls says, cutting across Mrs Pratchett.

'We agreed with everything you said,' her companion, a man with a perfectly round, bald head beams at me. 'You know, about Paradiso's.'

'Why don't you give us a song?' a tiny little woman with bright blue eyes pipes up in a bird-like voice. 'I can play piano if you want.'

'Oh yes, that would be lovely, dear,' a woman in a wheelchair smiles.

A murmur of agreement runs round the dayroom. I catch phrases like 'tremendous voice' and 'She's going to be a star,' and it's my turn to be gripped by panic.

'So what do you say, kid?' the man with the mop of silver hair demands. 'Are you going to give us a treat? Brighten our dull old days?'

I look round the room. A sea of wrinkled, bright-eyed faces stares back. My stomach clenches. I really don't know what to do! I look to Dad, but he gives me an *It's-up-to-you* shrug.

'I'm . . . s-s-sorry,' I stammer, my voice tiny. 'I've given up singing. I'm never going to sing again.'

A sigh of disappointment fills the room, followed by a slow muttering. Then an ancient, tiny woman stands up shakily.

'My name is Peggy Miller,' she says, her voice amazingly young and strong. 'I'm ninety-nine years old and, the Good Lord willing, I'll be a hundred very soon. And if there's one thing I've learned in life, young lady, it's this: if you've been given a talent – and you have, my dear – then it's your *duty* to use it, to do your best with it. You don't just owe it to yourself. You owe it to others too. Otherwise,' she pauses and fixes me with a stare so fierce I'm sure she can see right into my soul, 'you'll get to my age and you'll wonder, *Why didn't I do what I was put on this earth to do? Why didn't I fulfil my destiny?*'

A ripple of applause ensues, accompanied by mutterings of 'Peggy's right, you know,' and 'Couldn't have put it better myself.'

And I don't know what to say[17] – when thankfully a gong sounds somewhere nearby.

'Time for tea and cakes!' Mrs Pratchett announces with a quick double-clap of her hands. 'So we'll have to postpone the pleasure of a sing-along until another time. Everyone through to the dining hall. Hurry hurry!'

There's a fair amount of grumbling, but thankfully the lure of cake outweighs the desire to hear me sing. Digby and Dad swing back into *politician-in-public* mode, each grabbing a wheelchaired resident and making off with them.

The man with the mop of silver hair homes in on me. 'You sing your songs, lassie,' he says. 'And come back and see us when you're famous.'

I smile shakily. What's the point in telling him that I'm not going to be famous? That a whole herd of wild elephants couldn't drag me up on stage and make me sing again. After all, once I go he'll probably forget all about me.

While Dad and Digby and the others scoff cakes

[17] A new and not very nice experience!

in the dining hall I keep a low profile until it's time to leave.

As we head towards the exit, the old dear who made a dash for the door on our arrival eyes me. For a split second I think of holding the security door open as I pass through, of letting her make her bid for freedom, of cheering her on as she goes sprinting down the path on her little old-lady legs. Then Dad catches my eye. And I know it's more than my life's worth.

So I give her a little wave and let the door slide silently shut behind me.

18

The next day at school, no one says anything more about the charity concert idea. Yet for some inexplicably infuriating reason I can think about nothing else! It's partly cos of what the old lady at the home said – you know, about using my talent. And partly cos I suspect the rest of Eco Club's disappointed in me, that they think I'm being selfish, that I'm letting Taslima down. I mean, if someone would actually come out and SAY that, then I could put my case, justify my position. I could maybe even come up with another idea for raising money. Though, to be honest, I don't have one. Yet.

All day it's been incredibly warm. Clouds have been gathering and the sky's been growing ever darker. 'A storm will clear the air,' Miss Peabody said just before the bell rang. 'But let's hope you all get home safely first.'

As I hurry towards the side gate, Twig's sitting on the wall, waiting.

'Hi!' he says, leaping down and falling into step beside me like he's never been away.

'Hi!' I reply quietly.

'So how are things?'

'Not great.'

'So,' he says playfully. 'I go away for a few days and your life falls apart.'

'You could have phoned.'

'Actually, I was going to, but I couldn't get a signal. Mum lives in the middle of nowhere. She doesn't have a landline or Internet. But I did send a carrier pigeon.' He smiles at me through his flop of hair. 'Didn't you get my message?'

'Uh uh,' I shake my head. 'It must've got lost. So what did this message say?'

Twig turns and walks backwards so he's facing me, then he makes these silly pigeon sounds.

'Sorry, I don't speak pigeon. Can you translate?' Despite myself a smile twitches at the corners of my mouth.

'Certainly,' Twig grins. 'It said, "Twig's been thinking about things while he was away. He says you must never give up singing"'

'Yeah, well, the message has come too late,' I say quietly.

We walk on in silence for a few minutes, above us the sky an ominous brown-black.

'Megan told me about the idea for the fundraising concert,' Twig says. 'And I think you should do it.'

'Look, Twig. Can we talk about something else?' I snap.

'But I don't understand!' He throws his hands up in exasperation. 'Why won't you do the charity gig?'

'What is there to understand?' Frustration wells up inside me. 'It's simple. I tried singing. It didn't work out. End of story.'

Twig jumps in front of me and blocks my path. I step to the right. He steps to the right. I step to the left. He steps to the left.

'Are you going to let me past?'

'If you answer one question . . .' Twig holds my gaze. 'What didn't work out?'

'Everything!' I explode. 'Surely I don't have to tell *you* of all people! You were there! Y-Generation are NOT going to sign me and NEITHER is anyone else. Paradiso's have seen to that. I can't take on a huge multinational. So that's it. Like I told you before, I've given up singing. Anyway, there are TONS of other things I can do.'

'But singing isn't just about recording deals,' Twig counters. 'It's about people hearing your songs. Don't you see, if you give up, if you won't even sing for a charity gig, then you're letting Paradiso's beat you! I can't believe you're just rolling over!'

Twig's words hit me hard. I can see what he's saying. What's worse, I know, deep down, he's right.

'Look, it doesn't matter now,' I mutter as the first

fat drops of rain splat on to the path and a wind blows up as if from nowhere.

'What's your name?' Twig asks sharply.

'That's a silly question. You *know* my name!'

'Just say it!'

'Sassy,' I reply. 'My name is Sassy.'

'Well, maybe you should try to live up to it! Look it up in the dictionary when you get home. Some-one who was *really* sassy would do the fundraising concert. Someone who was *really* sassy would get up on that stage and sing. Don't you see, you need to prove to organizations like Paradiso's that they might have all the money, they might have all the power, but they can't silence you. They can't silence any of us!'

'OK,' I bridle, 'since *you* feel so strongly about it, then YOU get up on stage and do the concert. Why does it have to be me?'

Gently Twig touches my cheek, forcing me to look into his eyes. 'Cos you're the one with the voice,' he says softly as the rain falls heavier around us. 'You're the one with the songs. Agree to do the concert and I promise I'll do everything I can to help. Megan and Cordelia will do what they can. Everyone will. But *you're* the only one that can get kids to buy tickets. *You're* the one they want to hear.'

I'm trying not to listen, but even so the meaning of Twig's words filters through. And I remember what the old lady in the care home said: '*You'll get to my age and you'll wonder, "Why didn't I do what I was put on this earth to do? Why didn't I fulfil my destiny?"'*

'I can't,' I say stubbornly.

'Why not?' Twig fires back at me.

'Because!'

'Because what?' He looks deep into my eyes.

'Because . . .' I search for something I can say that will make him back off, leave me alone. 'Because . . . I . . . I don't have a guitar any more.'

'So that's your excuse?' Twig snorts.

'Yeah. If that's how you want to see it, that's my excuse. No guitar. No concert! OK?'

Something flits across Twig's face. Something I can't quite place. 'So if you had a guitar you'd do the concert?' he shouts above the wind that's coming in big angry gusts now.

And I'm about to say, *Well done, you've got it –* when he grabs me, kisses me on the nose, then turns and runs away.

BOYS! AAAAARGH! Honestly. They are SERIOUSLY WEIRD!

19

This is just not my day!

By the time I get home I'm soggy-sodden-soaking wet. And there's a note from Mum saying she's had to go out and help at Cathy's Totally Scrumptious Cake Cafe (AGAIN)! Dad is in Edinburgh with Digby, Pip has gone to a friend's straight from school and – can you believe it? – just when I desperately need some comfort food, there's NOT ONE home-made cake or brownie or tray-bake anywhere in the house. Honestly! My mother is neglecting her maternal duties since she started 'giving Cathy a hand'. She's giving her more than a hand! She's also giving her all the cakes that used to be kept in the fridge for yours truly and her little sis – a sorry state of affairs, which I for one, find totally intolerable!

I make do with a brace of ancient Jammie Dodgers and a cracked Bourbon cream scavenged from the bottom of the biscuit tin, grab a big glass of milk, wander through to the living room and switch on *News 24* – just as a bulletin comes in live from Pakistan. There have been more tremors in the earthquake area, the newsreader announces, as fresh images of devastation appear behind him. I know it's foolish, but even so, I lean forward and scour the screen, just in case I catch a glimpse of Taslima.

Then an aid worker comes on. Behind him a group of men dig through the rubble of a collapsed school. The news reporter says they believe there are survivors still trapped beneath the masonry. Several ambulances sit with their lights flashing.

'We know from previous earthquakes that people can survive in air pockets for days, sometimes weeks, if they have water and food in reach. But we need more aid, and we need it now,' the aid worker says passionately. 'Thousands have been killed and those who've survived are living rough on the mountainsides. In some ways the humanitarian crisis is just beginning. We urgently need tents and blankets. Water sources are polluted from burst sewer pipes, so we need water purification tablets. I appeal to all of you to help. Send your donations to the disaster relief fund. We can save hundreds, maybe even thousands of lives, but we need your money!'

Troubled, I flick the TV off and sit staring at the blank screen. The storm Miss Peabody predicted is in full flow now, the rain rattling angrily off the windows. I imagine being out on a mountainside, with no protection, nowhere safe to shelter. Twig's right. Kids at school *would* pay for tickets for a concert. Megan and Cordelia and Sindi-Sue – and even Magnus and Beano – would all rally round and do their bit. All I need to do is agree to sing.

I go into Dad's computer cupboard and press a button. The computer whirrs into life. I click on the online dictionary and punch in my name. S-A-S-S-Y. It comes up right away. *SASSY* |sæsɪ| *adjective – lively, bold, full of spirit.*

I sit staring at the screen. Thinking. I guess if I give up singing cos Y-Generation won't sign me, then I'm not being true to my name. I'm being a wimp. A walkover. I'm letting Paradiso's win. And deep down I know there's a tiny voice trying to be heard, a tiny sassy voice, whispering: *Actually, Sassy, you do want to sing again, you're just being stubborn and wrongheaded.*

But then again I tell myself OUT LOUD[18] so I can drown the little voice out: 'IF YOU WERE MEANT TO SING, THEN Y-GENERATION WOULD HAVE SIGNED YOU!'

All irritated and out of sorts I wander upstairs and open the door to my room. Oh no! I must have left the window open this morning. The

[18] I so wish Taslima was around. Surely talking out loud to yourself must be an early sign of madness!!!

rain-soaked curtains are billowing and flapping as the storm blows in. I dash across and slam the window shut just as a flash of lightning splits the sky. And that's when I see it. Propped against my desk.

At first I can't believe my eyes. It's a guitar! And not just any guitar. It's MY guitar! A massive peal of thunder booms right above the house. I stare open-mouthed as another lightning flash floods the room, momentarily blinding me. When my eyes readjust I half expect the guitar to have disappeared, like it was an illusion, a trick of the brain, something Cordelia had conjured up with one of her spells.

But it's still there! I rush over and pick it up. Solid and real and . . . err . . . damp. Grabbing a T-shirt, grinning insanely, I wipe it dry. Then I strum a few times and suddenly, despite all my resolutions about never wanting to sing again, I'm so happy I could cry!

And I'm wondering how on earth it got there, when I realize there's a label tied round its neck. On it a carefully handwritten message:

If you think you are too small to make a difference,
try sleeping with a mosquito
The Dalai Lama[19]

[19] Buddhist monk dude from Tibet. Non-violent. Spends his whole life spreading good karma.

I read and re-read the words. Until finally I understand.

With tears in my eyes, sniffing and smiling, all at the same time, I tune my guitar. As I strum its strings, it vibrates against me, like a cat purring contentedly. I bend over and kiss its frets, and that's when I notice that Twig's friendship bracelet – the old, faded, broken one – has gone. In its place is a fresh one, all beautifully woven in golds and purples – my fave colours, my lucky colours.

I take it off and tie it round my wrist. Twig's right. I might be small, but like a mosquito, I can be effective.

And I'm not going to let bullies like Paradiso's stop me.

20

Half an hour later the storm has blown itself out
and the sun bursts through the clouds, edging them
with silver.

I set my guitar on its stand, all dried and tuned,
then clatter downstairs and hurry into the garage.
I drag my bike out and furiously pedal round
to Twig's. As I fly along the rain-soaked, sun-
drenched streets, steam rises around me in magic
wispy clouds. The air smells green and fresh.
Everything's glistening. Like the whole world's
beautiful and new!

At Twig's house I drop my bike in the drive and
run towards the door – then stop in my tracks as
something cracks off my skull. A nut! I look up into
the tree where Twig likes to sit, but there's no bright
face grinning down. I squeal and rub my head as
another nut bounces off it.

'So you found it?' Twig's hanging out of an
upstairs window, his hair flopping forward.

'Yeah, I did. Thanks!' I beam up at him.

'Wait there!' he shouts and seconds later he opens the door.

'How did you do it? I mean, why?' I splutter.

Twig shrugs. 'When Megan told me you'd taken your guitar to the Oxfam shop, I knew you'd done the wrong thing. So I thought I'd better buy it before anyone else did. I guessed you'd want it eventually.'

'So how come you knew I'd done the wrong thing before I did?' I ask, confused, as I follow him through to the kitchen.

Twig smiles and takes two glasses from the cupboard. 'Good friends look out for each other,' he says as he pours out some mango juice. 'You're too good a singer – and a songwriter – to give it all up.'

'Look, I owe you, Twig. Whatever it cost to buy the guitar at Oxfam, I'll pay you back.'

Twig leans against the worktop and passes me a glass. 'You don't need to pay. Not in money, anyway . . . Maybe you could just do something for me instead?' He pushes his hair back from his face and smiles cheekily. For a moment I think he's going to ask me to kiss him, and that's when an awful realization dawns on me – the way things have been between us recently, I'm not sure that I *want* to.

'So this favour,' I ask, taking a step back. 'What were you thinking of?'

He looks into my face, his eyes shining, eager.

'Do the fundraising concert, Sassy. Sing up on stage again. You've no excuse now you've got your guitar back.'

'Yeah, well, that's what I think too,' I smile. 'You're right. I should do it.'

'Fantastic!' Twig raises his glass to chink with mine. 'Megan says there're tons of folk willing to muck in. And Sassy –' He takes a step closer and I can't step back cos the wall's right behind me. 'I think you're great.' His breath flutters against my cheek and I just know he's about to kiss me when the door bursts open and Megan comes bouncing into the kitchen.

'Ooooops!' she squeals, retreating back through the door. 'Omigod! Sorree!'

'Don't go, Megan!' I shout, nimbly stepping round Twig and going after her. Who would have thought? For once I am actually relieved to be interrupted by Megan!

Pleased, she bounces back into the room.

'Good news!' I grin. 'Twig got me my guitar back. So it looks like we can do the concert. If everyone still wants to, that is.'

'WHOOP!' Megan squeals, throwing her arms round me in a big hug. 'That's great news! Break open the pink lemonade! Let's celebrate!'

21

From <u>sassywilde@gmail.com</u>
To <u>professortas@yahoo.com</u>

Hi Tas!

Maybe you won't get to read this till you come home, cos there's maybe no Internet where you are. Maybe not even any electricity. I AM SO WORRIED ABOUT YOU! But at least when you do read this you'll know we've all been thinking about you.

Just wanted you to know too that even tho I'm never gonna be a big star now, me and some others (Cordelia, Megan, Midge, Twig, Magnus, Sindi-Sue and Beano) are gonna do a lunchtime concert at school to raise money to send to the Earthquake Appeal Fund.

I know it's not a HUGE thing to do to help, but it's all we can think of.

So be careful, Tas. I miss you lots. Remember, you're my personal therapist, and, hey, do I need therapy. I'm in such a muddle about Twig, like you wouldn't believe. I suppose it might just be a weird patch we're going through. I so need you to sort out my head. Especially cos I don't know what to do about Phoenix either. He's sent me a card and texted and I think he'd like to stay in touch . . . And so would I!

Cordelia says she's cast a BIG magic spell to keep you safe. She's been sending you psychic good luck messages too.

Can't wait to hear from you – and for you to come home. Please tell your mum I am trying my ultra-bestest to be a good person.

Love ya Loads! BFF!
Sassy xxx :o)
PS Brewster sends a big doggy kiss too.

I click Send, and before I go to sleep I devise a plan for getting the school fundraising concert off the ground. First thing tomorrow morning, before Registration even starts, I will go and see Smollett. I'll explain about Tas and the earthquake and how Eco Club wants to raise money to help, and how we figure the best way is a lunchtime concert, so all *he* has to do is let us have the use of the school hall. We can even try to get a piece in the local paper. *STRATHCARRON HIGH STUDENTS DO CHARITY GIG*-type thing. And maybe even a spot on local radio. Which, I will point out, would all be very good for the reputation of the school. So he's bound to say yes.

22

Aaaargh! What is wrong with my family! First I can't get into the shower this morning cos Pip beats me to it, which means I have to wait YONKS while she carries out her morning beauty routine.

'I don't want to end up with a face like a dried sultana by the time I'm fifteen,' she protests when I try to drag her out. 'Which is what will happen to *you* cos you don't follow a proper facial care routine!'

It is almost quarter past eight before she flounces out on her silly kitten-heel mules and I at last get into the shower.

Then, when I go into The Pig Pen[20] to pick my clean school shirt off the floor – where I have EVERY right to leave it overnight if I want to – Mrs Houdini is asleep on it. Which would be fine

[20] Pip has started up a new design-a-sign business. She actually got Dad to PAY for making signs for all the rooms in our house. My room's now The Pig Pen. Hers is The Pink Palace.

if it was just a bit warm, hairy and hamster-smelly – but she's PEED on it!

Of course, I run downstairs screaming to Mum, who is sitting writing out a cake recipe from *Cakes in Two Shakes* – only to discover she put ALL my other shirts in the wash last night and they are still sodden wet in the machine.

'Put on a T-shirt,' Mum says calmly. 'Look, I'll write you a note.' She tears another sheet from her writing pad. 'Then if anyone says anything about you not wearing a proper school shirt, they'll know it's not your fault. OK? Crisis over?'

But the crisis isn't over. Cos my dad, instead of putting on his frilly apron and serving up coffee and smoothies and toast like a NORMAL dad would, is running around crazily looking for some important papers he's lost. Honestly. It's one thing me not being able to find things in the morning, like a missing sock or shoe or a science workbook, but you'd think a fully-grown parental could be a bit better organized.

In the end I pull on my *SAVE THE PLANET – IT'S THE ONLY ONE WE'VE GOT* T-shirt, gulp down a glass of milk, grab the note Mum wrote, and rocket out the door.

So much for hoping to get in early before registration, I think as I sprint towards the school. With all the panic over my shirt, I am now not only NOT early, I am HORRENDOUSLY late.

As soon as I enter the playground Lanky Lovelace – who absolutely hates me – swoops, his tiny red shorts glowing in the early morning sunshine.

'OK, OK, no sweat,' I say as he directs me to join the other latecomers waiting at the school office. 'I was wanting to see Mr Smollett anyway, thank you.' He glowers at me and I feel a little rush of delight that I've annoyed him by being polite.

At the glass window of the school office I tag on at the end of a straggle of latecomers, all yawning and scratching themselves. Most of them look like they could do with a dose of Pip's skin-freshening regime. The girl in front of me glances sleepily at my T-shirt and smiles.

One by one they sign the late register, take a slip and disappear to their registration classes. But when I get to the front of the queue, I ring the bell. Miss Crump frowns at me over her morning cuppa, then slowly comes over and even more slowly slides the glass window open.

'I'd like to see Mr Smollett, please,' I say with my best smile. 'It's important. And urgent.'

Miss Crump narrows her dead-fish eyes. 'Take a seat and I'll see if he's free,' she says snippily. Then she disappears.

Twenty minutes later I'm still waiting and getting a horrible feeling of *déjà vu*. I wiggle my toes to stave off premature deep vein thrombosis.

Twenty-two minutes later Miss Crump at last informs me I can go through to the Head's office.

I stand up carefully and am secretly pleased that this time the chair doesn't make a disgusting noise. For the first time today things are starting to work in my favour.

Smollett looks up from his desk as I enter, and I'm about to launch into my spiel about the concert and how we need the hall, when his scowl stops me.

'What is THAT you're wearing?' he says in a low growl.

I glance down at my T-shirt. 'Oh, there was a problem with my school shirt, Sir. The hamster . . . errr . . . peed . . . on the last clean one and Mum had only gone and put all the rest in the wash last night so they were totally sodden wet.' Suddenly I remember the note. I dig it from my pocket and hand it over with a flourish.

As Smollett opens it and smoothes it out his frown deepens. 'Is this your idea of a joke?' he says. 'Or is it some kind of dare?'

'No,' I say, my voice faltering. 'It's a note from my mum. About my shirt.'

'Really?' he says, placing the open note in front of me. Quickly I scan the first few words.

SWEET LOVE CAKES
4 eggs
8 oz flour
8 oz butter
vanilla essence . . .

'Ooops!' All the blood in my body rushes up to my face as, embarrassed, I snatch the note back. 'Looks like I brought the wrong note, Sir. But the thing is, the real reason I'm here is, well, you know how there's been that earthquake in Pakistan? Well, my friend Taslima, she's in my class, she's gone out there with her mum and we – that is Eco Club – we want to do our bit to help so we're gonna do this fundraising concert thing and I'm gonna sing, so we wanted to know if we could have the school hall some lunchtime –'

'Stop right there!' Smollett booms, getting up out of his seat. 'You want to know if you can have the school hall one lunchtime?'

'Yes. That's it,' I confirm with a hopeful smile. 'Preferably in the next week.'

'Let me get this right,' he says, pacing back and forth behind his desk. 'You, Sassy Wilde, a girl who led a walk-out from this school not two months ago, a girl who came in late this morning – oh yes, I saw you from my window! A girl who constantly flouts the school uniform rules, who almost caused a riot in assembly, who lied to me about having a note from her mother . . . *You* want me to let you use the school hall so you can get up on stage and sing your atrocious pop songs?'

For a brief second I think about putting him right on the 'pop' songs bit. But his baldy head's glowing like a radioactive radish. I'm no nurse, but

I suspect he has high blood pressure and his cranium is about to explode.

'Yes, Sir.' I nod. 'That's about it. But it is for a good cause.'

It's after lunch before I get out of the sin bin.

It was not a pleasant experience. A horrible little First Year boy pinged paper bullets at me every time the teacher wasn't looking. And a Fourth Year with a shaved head sent me a note saying he'd like me to be his girlfriend and would I meet him at lunchtime behind the PE block.

As if that wasn't bad enough, all I had to look forward to on my release was the prospect of explaining to my friends that I'd completely blown our chances of ever getting the school hall.

As soon as I appear in class everyone flocks round me to find out how on earth I ended up in such BIG trouble. They listen in silence as I detail the trials and tribulations of my day so far.

'What sort of idiot are you?' Magnus explodes. 'We were all supposed to be doing this concert thing together. The whole Eco Club. You should've waited and spoken to the rest of us. *I* could've asked Smollett for the school hall, then we would've got it, no problem.'

'Hey, that's not fair,' Cordelia counters him with a flash of her eyes. 'Sassy did what she did for the right reasons.'

'Yeah, but let's face it, Magnus has a point,' I mumble, biting my lip to stop it quivering. 'Look at him. Everything about him's perfect. He gets straight As. Always has a perfect uniform. Never gets into trouble. A star pupil. He's right. If *he'd* asked, Smollett would've said yes. I'm sorry. I guess I just got over-enthusiastic. I've blown it.'

Sindi-Sue puts a comforting arm round me and fires Magnus a look. 'I don't think you should be so mean to Sassy,' she says quietly. 'She was trying to do the right thing.'

'OK, OK!' Magnus takes a deep breath and rolls his eyes. 'I'm sorry, Sass. I didn't mean to upset you.'

'Like, am I totally missin' somefin' here?' Midge pops up from under his desk. 'Like, is the school hall the *only* hall in town?'

Cordelia looks at Midge, her green eyes wide with amazement. 'You're a genius, Midge!' she exclaims. 'Of course there's another hall. The TOWN hall! Maybe we could get the town hall!'

'Yeah, that would be awesome,' Sindi-Sue says, suddenly excited. 'Then we could do it in the evening, like on a Friday or Saturday, and get tons more peeps. It could be like a REAL concert. We could all get dressed up and everything.'

'Errr . . . I don't want to be the one to put a downer on things,' Magnus butts in. 'But you really think they're going to let a bunch of kids hire the town hall?'

Everyone's silent for a moment. Then Megan pipes up, 'Yes! I bet they will – if Sassy's dad asks! I mean, he's our MP, isn't he? That's got to be worth something.'

'So will your dad do it, Sassy?' Magnus says and everyone turns to stare at me.

'Course he will.' I try to sound more confident than I feel. 'Why on earth wouldn't he?'

23

Twig's not at the school gate today, which is just as well, cos I'm a Girl on a Mission. And a G on an M does not have time for a love life, especially one that's turned a bit complicated. I desperately need to prove to my friends that I can do something right. The sooner I get home, the sooner I can get Dad to phone the town hall.

But when I get home, Dad's 'office' door is firmly shut, and on it in huge black letters it says,

MP AT WORK – DO NOT DISTURB!

Which is a pretty daft thing for an MP to put on his door! I mean, surely he'd want to know if, say, Tobermory had been hit by a tsunami, or the Third World War had broken out in Poland or . . . the Queen had popped her royal clogs?

So I'm about to burst in and say that I've got a bit of an emergency, i.e. I need him to book the town hall for the Earthquake Relief Fund concert right away – when Pip materializes at my side.

'There's no point,' she says. 'He's not there. I

just checked. We have an absent father. And it's worse!' She waves a piece of paper under my nose. 'This note I just found on the kitchen table says Mum won't be home tonight to make our tea.' Pip looks at her reflection in the hall mirror. 'I mean, I used to worry about getting too FAT, but since Mum started helping Cathy at the cake shop I swear I'm getting that malny-trishin thingy.'

'M-A-L-N-U-T-R-I-T-I-O-N,' I spell for her. 'And now you come to mention it, Pip, you're absolutely right. There's hardly been a cake or cookie in the house this past week. We are seriously at risk of becoming neglected children. But I don't suppose there's much we can do. Not till our delinquent parentals come home!'

While I wait for Dad to get back, I find what grub I can for me and Pip, then up in my room I start getting together a playlist of as many songs as possible. I've been writing my own songs for over a year now, so fortunately I've got quite a few.

I'm happily belting out 'My Imaginary Friend's Not Sweet' to see if it's good enough for the concert, when I hear the front door open. There's a familiar clatter as Dad chucks his car keys on the hall table. Quickly I lay my guitar on my bed and go thundering downstairs, but not before Pip's got Dad cornered, holding out an empty bowl, her eyes big and round like an exceptionally pretty Oliver Twist.

'What on earth's the problem?' Dad stares at the bowl, bewildered.

'I'm hungry, Dad,' Pip looks up at him, her lip quivering. 'Mum's not coming home till later, so I thought you might like to cook for us? As a special treat?'

I'm about to put in my much more simple request – one quick phone call to the town hall – when Dad runs a hand through his hair in exasperation. 'Sorry, Pip, but those important papers I couldn't find this morning are *still* missing. NOTHING else can be done till I find them!'

'Tell you what,' Pip says brightly, as she pops her bowl on the hall table. 'Me and Sassy will help you find your missing papers, *then* you make our tea. Deal?' She reaches her tiny red-nailed fingers out and Dad takes her hand and shakes.

'It's a deal, princess. And hopefully you won't die of starvation before they turn up. They really are very important.'

As we follow Dad and Digby I have a flash of the future: *I find Dad's Very Important Papers, and he's so overcome with gratitude he immediately calls the town hall and books it for the concert.*

But when I see inside the dining room my jaw drops open in horror. Honestly, it's like there's been a whirlwind in a paper factory!

'Errr . . . I'm afraid we got into a bit of a muddle earlier . . .' Digby says apologetically.

'You still don't have a filing system?' I gasp.

'We're waiting for the filing cabinets to be delivered,' Dad explains. 'And yes, there is a system. Or at least there was. Before we started to look for the papers. I absolutely need them for a meeting first thing tomorrow morning.'

'OK,' I say, taking charge. (It's pretty obvious someone has to!) 'Let's work out a strategy, a *modus operandi*.'[21] Digby looks impressed, but already Pip's distracted. She's found a rather attractive lime green highlighter and is trying it out, doodling a row of smiley faces along the top of a letter. 'There's four of us. Right? There are four corners in the room. Right? We can each take a corner and work in towards the centre. That way, if the papers are here, we're sure to find them.'

Dad bites his lip and nods. 'Sounds like a plan,' he says. 'I really appreciate this, girls. In fact, find the missing papers and we can get takeaway pizzas for tea if you like.'

Pip and I whoop with delight. We LOVE takeaway pizzas.

'And there's a small favour I need too . . .' I say quickly as I choose a corner to start from. 'Me and my friends want to do a fundraising concert for the earthquake disaster. But we need

[21] I learned that from Tas. It's Latin for 'way of doing things'.

the town hall. So would you call them for us? Tonight?'

'Sassy,' Dad says, 'you find my missing papers and I'll call the Queen Mother for you.'

'Ahem,' Digby interrupts quietly. 'She's dead.'

'Well, in that case I'll call the Queen,' Dad smiles.

'No need,' I grin, pushing my sleeves up, ready for some hard graft. 'Just call the town hall, see if you can book it for as soon as possible. That will be great.' Whoop! I can't believe it was so easy to get Dad onside!

'So,' says Pip, putting the highlighter down and choosing the far corner by the shredding machine. 'Tell us *exactly* what we're looking for.'

'Right,' says Dad. 'The papers we're looking for are quite distinctive. For a start, they're pink –'

'Quite a pretty shade, actually,' Digby adds.

'PINK?!' Pip gasps.

Dad and Digby stare at Pip. Her face blushes, well, pink. Then deepens to raspberry.

Dad's eyes narrow. 'Oh no, Pip. You've done something with the papers, haven't you?'

She clamps her mouth tight shut and shakes her head. Dad glances at Pip's highlighter doodles.

'You haven't used them to draw on, have you?' Digby asks, ashen-faced.

Pip shakes her head. 'Worse than that,' she mumbles.

'You've cut them up into paper dolls?' Dad ventures.

'Worse than that,' Pip says, her voice a tiny whisper. She throws me a look, but I'm stunned into silence. Something that doesn't happen very often.

'You still have the papers, then?' Hope flickers in Digby's eyes.

Pip nods and smiles. Digby thinks it's a smile that means everything's going to be fine. But I recognize it as a smile of pain, a smile that means things are worse than you could ever imagine. A smile that says, *Please don't kill me when I tell you the truth.*

'So can we have them back?' Digby makes for the door. 'Whatever she's done, Angus,' he calls over his shoulder as he bounds upstairs two-at-a-time, 'I'm sure we can salvage them.'

We all follow Digby into Pip's room. Digby looks around The Pink Palace. 'OK, Pip,' he smiles encouragingly. 'Don't worry. We're not going to be angry. Where are the papers?'

Pip goes over to her hamster cage. Dad follows, his smile fading. He peers inside. Mrs Houdini peers back. And that's when Dad realizes the awful truth.

'*PIP!*' he gasps. 'How could you? You've used important government papers to line the floor of your hamster cage!'

Angrily, Dad unclips the cage door, just as a dark pink stain spreads from underneath Mrs Houdini across the last unsoiled few centimetres, turning them as dark a shade of puce as Dad's face.

'Do you mind!' Pip snaps, angrily pushing Dad aside. 'You've frightened Mrs Houdini!' She puts her hand in the open cage door, gently pushes Mrs Houdini to one side and, in a flurry of wood shavings and tiny hamster poo, she tugs out the sodden pink papers and thrusts them at Dad. 'Here! You can have your stinky papers!'

Which is when Dad loses it. 'Pip! You're *grounded*!' he splutters, his voice higher-pitched than a baby Houdini's. 'For a week! And there will be no pizza for you tonight, young lady. You can be sure of that!'

Tears spring up in Pip's eyes. For a split second I think of sneaking out of the door and disappearing. A kind of tactical withdrawal from the battlefield. Maybe if Pip takes all the blame, Dad might still call the town hall. Maybe . . .

But I can't do it. It wouldn't be fair. After all, Pip didn't use the papers to line the hamster cage. I did.

'It's not Pip to blame,' I pipe up as my heart plummets. 'Pip had nothing to do with it. *I* used the pink paper. When I was doing one of my good deeds.' I sigh heavily. There goes any chance of us getting the town hall. Struggling not to burst into tears, I blurt, 'But it's not my fault – not totally! The papers were sitting on the pile for shredding.

If you had a proper filing system, things like this wouldn't happen, would they?'

Dad turns towards me, his face still puce. Digby takes the soiled papers from his hand and disappears downstairs with them. A faint stink of hamster pee lingers. Pip slips silently across the room, stands shoulder to shoulder with me like she's saying, *We're both in this together.* As she slips her hand into mine, I squeeze it gratefully. Then Dad takes a deep breath.

'You were doing a good deed?' he repeats slowly, like he's trying to stop himself self-igniting.

I nod. Tears sting the backs of my eyes and I bite my lip to hold them back.

Dad looks at Pip and me for a moment longer. 'OK,' he sighs at last. 'Maybe you're right, Sassy. We do need a proper filing system, and my office shouldn't be in the house, so I have to take some of the blame. But there's something I want both of you to understand. As long as the dining room is my office, you must *never* go in there without permission. OK?'

Pip rushes over to Dad and gives him a big hug.

'So, Sassy,' he says evenly. 'How about another good turn, eh? Do you think you could order the pizzas?'

Just then the doorbell rings and Pip goes skipping off to answer it.

'So what about the town hall, Dad?' I say in a

tiny voice. 'Will you call them? I don't mind not having pizza if you'll do that instead. In fact I don't mind not eating for a week.'

Dad eyeballs me like he's looking into my soul. Pip returns from answering the door and Cordelia's with her. The atmosphere's so tense they stand in the doorway unsure whether or not to come any further.

Dad looks from me to Cordelia, pushes his glasses up on top of his head and narrows his eyes. 'Tell you what, I'll phone the town hall for you – if *you* do something for me.'

'OK, OK!' I say. 'Whatever – shredding papers, licking envelopes, sticking on stamps, delivering leaflets – I'll do it!'

'And I'll help!' Cordelia offers enthusiastically. 'We really do want to do the concert.'

'So you'll do anything?' Dad asks.

'Absolutely,' I nod.

'Good! That's what I hoped you'd say,' Dad says, and there's something about the glint in his eye that makes me wonder what kind of bargain we've struck.

24

'We've had the cycle safety gear redesigned. I think you're going to like it this time.' Dad explains as he rummages in a box and tugs out a bright orange waistcoat, polka-dotted with lemon reflectors. 'See? It's now super-sexy cycle safety gear!'

'The orange is fluorescent in the dark,' Digby says animatedly. 'And the yellow reflectors are . . . well . . . reflective. I passed on what you said, Sassy, about the last version being too shapeless and baggy, so the designers have come up with this rather fetching luminous lime belt. See, you can cinch it in at the waist. Oh, and they've taken the flashing light off the top of the helmet and put one on each side instead.'

'That's . . . er . . . totally awesome,' Cordelia gasps.

'Yeah, Dad. Awesome! Wicked! Super!' I lie. Honestly I can't believe how wrong grown-ups get it sometimes. It's honking! 'You can quote me on that if you want. So now will you phone the town hall?'

'I'm glad you like it so much,' Dad beams. 'Here's the deal. *I'll* phone the town hall, while *you* model the new cycle gear.' Dad pulls another super-sexy cycle safety waistcoat from the box. 'We need some photos for the press. So grab a couple of bikes from the garage. Digby's got the camera. It will only take a few minutes.'

Dad lied about the 'few minutes' bit.

Digby couldn't get the camera to work properly and in the end me and Cordelia had to hang about in the street for more than half an hour – dressed in Dad's stupid cycle gear!

Of course, Cordelia looked fantastic. I don't know how she does it![22] But me? Well, I looked an absolute dork. I will be UTTERLY humiliated if the photos ever appear anywhere.

'Never mind,' Cordelia says cheerily. 'Just think of all that good karma you're storing up by helping your dad out.'

By the time we finish, Mum has come home, the takeaway pizzas have arrived and Dad has phoned the town hall.

'Bad news,' he says as we tug the waistcoats off. 'Sorry, girls. But the hall's all booked up. The first available date's in three months' time. It's a shame, but I think that's the end of your concert idea.'

[22] Maybe she does have magic powers?!

'But we really wanted to raise money for the earthquake,' I groan.

'And tons of kids wanted to hear Sassy sing. They're going to be so disappointed,' Cordelia sighs.

'Never mind, love,' Dad says. 'I'm sure you'll get other chances to sing. You've done your best.'

Ten minutes later Cordelia and me are tucking into the takeaway pizzas in the kitchen, comfort eating, and I'm moaning on to Cordelia about the whole karma thing not really working like I'd hoped it would, when Digby comes through, a watermelon smile splitting his face.

'Guess who that was on the phone?' he grins. 'Only the town hall! A wedding party for Saturday the fourteenth has just cancelled. The bride's changed her mind. The town hall wants to know if that's any use for your benefit gig?' He nicks an olive from Pip's pizza and pops it in his mouth.

'You mean Saturday as in one week from tomorrow Saturday?' Cordelia splutters through a mouthful of melted mozzarella.

Digby nods. 'And they said you can have the hall for free as it's for charity.'

'Yay! That's brilliant!' I wave my fork and acci- dentally splatter Brewster's nose with a blob of gherkin[23]. 'It's Friday now, so that gives us seven whole days to get organized.'

'We can email out invites,' Cordelia says, 'and stick up posters –'

'Excuse me, ladies,' Digby interrupts. 'The town hall's still on the phone. Is that a *yes* for Saturday week?'

'No!' I squawk.

Digby looks surprised.

'It's a *YES!! YES!! YES!!*' Cordelia and I squeal together, then we rush up to my room and text Megan, Sindi-Sue, Midge, Beano and Magnus: ☆ *TOWN HALL IS GO! – MEET MY PLACE – NOW* ☆. I'll let Twig know the good news by carrier pigeon. We're gonna need all hands on deck to get organized in time.

---

[23] Cordelia's idea. Try it! It's kinda cool.

25

Megan arrives first and Twig's with her. They're closely followed by Magnus, who knocks politely on the window like it's a classroom door!

Next, Beano's brown face peers through the leaves. He climbs in carefully, wary of tipping things over with his long legs. A text pings in from Midge to say he can't make it. Then the doorbell rings and I run down to answer it.

'Sorry, Sass,' Sindi-Sue says in a flurry of hairspray and perfume. 'Climbing trees really ain't my thing. Is it OK if I come in through the door?'

Minutes later we're all crammed into my room. Cordelia, Sindi-Sue and Megan sit cross-legged on the bed. Beano sinks on to the beanbag. Twig lounges on my rainbow rug with Brewster's head in his lap. Magnus perches on the chair at my desk.

'It's OK, Magnus. Relax!' Cordelia teases. 'He doesn't bite.'

'Who doesn't bite?' Sindi-Sue giggles. 'Twig or the dog?'

'Neither,' says Megan. 'They're both pussy cats, really.'

'Right,' I say, nabbing a space on the end of the bed. 'Here's the deal. The good news is we got the town hall –'

'So what's the bad news?' Magnus asks.

'The bad news is the date. All they have free is Saturday the fourteenth – a week tomorrow,' Cordelia explains.

'But we'll never get organized by then!' Magnus gasps. 'It's not like doing it at school. We'll need to advertise and stuff.'

'Omigod!' says Sindi-Sue, her mouth hanging open in an exaggerated pink gloss O. 'That's gonna be a bit of a rush!'

'But we have to do it soon anyway,' Cordelia points out. 'It *is* an emergency we're raising money for.'

'Yeah, but have you really thought this through?' Twig tickles Brewster's ears and he lollops over on to his back to get his tummy tickled too[24]. 'A lunchtime school concert is one thing – but asking people to come out for a gig – and expecting them to cough up money – you're gonna need more than a half-hour of songs and an acoustic guitar, Sassy.'

'Oh dear,' I say slowly. 'I didn't think of that . . .'

[24] Brewster, that is. Not Twig.

'Me neither,' Cordelia sighs. 'I guess we just got caught up in all the excitement . . .'

'So what are you peeps saying?' Sindi-Sue looks confused. 'Like, are we doing this benefit thingie or not?'

'I dunno,' Twig pushes back his flop of hair. 'Maybe if we had more time we could've got a band together –'

'A band?' I sit up. I know I'm probably grasping at straws, but as Confucius[25] he say, *When you're sinking fast, grasping a straw is the only sensible thing left to do.* 'That's a great idea. I don't suppose any of you guys know anyone who could be in it?'

'Actually, I play lead guitar,' Beano says quietly.

'And Twig plays electric fiddle,' Megan adds excitedly.

Twig throws her a *Why-did-you-say-that* look.

'Well, you do!' she protests. '*And* you're good. I should know. I have to listen to you every single night!'

Twig shifts uneasily. 'Yeah, but that's the point, Megan. It's a private thing. I play in my own room. For myself. Not for other people.'

'But you're way good enough to!' Megan exclaims. 'It would be awesome if you guys got a band together –'

[25] Ancient Chinese philosopher. Said lots of wise things. Though maybe not that!

'In a week?' Twig protests. 'I don't think so . . . But as you're so keen for me to play fiddle, why aren't you offering to play drums?'

'Do you play drums?' Magnus turns to Megan, his eyes wide with admiration. She blushes pink to the roots of her hair.

'Actually . . . no!' She throws Twig a killer look.

'But you *do* have a drum kit!' Twig insists. 'Up at the back of the garage. I've seen it. Under an old blanket.'

'That's not mine,' Megan blurts, a wobble in her voice. 'It was my dad's. He left it behind . . . you know . . . when he moved out. Mum couldn't bear to chuck it, so she shoved it up the back of the garage.'

'So is it still working?' Magnus asks, totally insensitive as always. I fire him a *Back-off-you are-treading-on-sensitive-territory* look, but in true Magnus style he completely misses it. 'Couldn't you dig it out, Megan? I mean playing drums can't be that hard, can it? You just have to whack them.'

I roll my eyes. The Magnus approach to music!

'Actually,' Megan retorts, 'I'm pretty good on drums. Dad taught me to play as soon as I could hold a drumstick. I even used to play with his band sometimes.'

'So what's your problem?' Magnus asks.

'The problem is, I don't want to!' Megan explodes. 'I haven't played since Dad left. So why don't you shut your stupid big mouth!'

Magnus looks baffled and hurt, like an over-excited pup that's just run slap-bang into a wall he thought was a door. I almost feel sorry for him.

'Hey, people!' Sindi-Sue flutters her fingers. 'Let's cool it, eh? Aren't we maybe losing sight of what we're actually in reality supposed to be doing here?'

'Sindi-Sue has a point,' Cordelia twirls a pencil in her fingers. 'We're either gonna do this gig and raise the money for the Earthquake Disaster Fund, or else we call the town hall, cancel the booking, forget all –'

She stops as Pip bursts into the room.

And I'm about to remind my little sis that she's supposed to KNOCK before entering The Pig Pen, when she shoves the phone at me.

'It's Taslima!' she gasps.

As I grab the phone, everyone falls silent. 'Taslima! Are you OK? Where are you?'

'Islamabad,' Taslima's voice crackles down the line. 'Listen, the phones are bad. We might get cut off. I got your email, Sass, and it cheered me up so much – you know – knowing you're doing a concert for the earthquake fund. Everything's such a mess here and there's so much needs doing. Mum's village is totally flattened and Aisya's in hospital with a broken leg and she wants me to say thank you to you all for raising money to help –'

The line clicks, then goes dead. Seconds later,

the dialling tone buzzes in my ear like a trapped bluebottle.

I press End Call and try 1471, hoping I'll get the number so I can call Tas back. But all I get is an automated message: *The number you requested is not available.*

We sit for several minutes in tense silence staring at the phone, willing it to ring again. Finally, we accept it's not going to.

Everyone listens solemnly as I repeat what Taslima said.

'Well, that's it. We have to do the concert now,' Cordelia says when I finish. 'I don't care how.'

'I agree,' says Sindi-Sue. 'Tas will be so disappointed when she comes back if she thinks we just gave up.'

'In that case, can someone tell me, do we have a band or not?' Magnus asks with an exasperated sigh.

'OK. Count me in. But on one condition.' Twig fixes Megan with a steely stare. 'I'll play fiddle, if my stepsis agrees to play drums.'

'I don't know,' Megan says, fidgeting with her bracelets. 'Dad's drum kit hasn't been used in ages. It might be all rusty by now –'

'But it's not!' Twig interrupts. 'I had the covers off when you were at school. It's in great nick.'

'Listen, Megan.' Magnus says quietly. 'Sorry if I upset you a minute ago. Thing is, I think you'd look really . . . cute . . . playing drums.' He gazes at her all puppy-eyed. Cordelia and Sindi-Sue exchange an *Are-you-thinking-what-I'm-thinking* smile.

'OK,' Megan blushes. 'I'll give it a go – for Tas. But don't expect me to be brilliant!'

'Don't expect any of us to be brilliant!' Twig laughs.

'Excuse me!' I object, picking up my guitar and strumming it softly. 'The rest of you might be rubbish (strum) but I for one (strum) am gonna be fantastic!'

'OK! OK!' Cordelia rummages among the clutter on my desk and finds a notebook. 'Let's make a plan of action. We can try out the band idea over the next couple of days, and if it doesn't work, we'll cancel the town hall and come up with another way to raise the money. But right now I need to know who's doing what.'

Ten minutes later we're all organized. Tomorrow's Saturday. So first rehearsal's in Megan's garage at ten. Magnus has got a swim-meet, but he'll be finished by twelve, then he'll make up a poster on his computer.

'I'll email something to you all later tomorrow,' Magnus says. 'Then everyone can forward it to all the people on their address list and ask them to do the same. That way we'll reach hundreds of people instantly.'

'Great idea!' Megan says. 'Not just a pretty face, then!' And Magnus's ears burn crimson!

'Don't we need a name for the band?' Beano asks, just when we think we've got everything under control.

'How about we call ourselves *Crazy Crew*?' I joke. 'I mean that's what we are, isn't it?'

'No,' says Magnus, frowning like he's working something out. 'You've already got a bit of profile, Sassy. People know your name. So we need to keep it in. I'll put a link on the e-poster to your online video clip too.'

'Clips, actually,' Twig says quietly. 'I uploaded that Wiccaman TV bit the other day. It's had quite a lot of hits.' He smiles shyly at me and I smile back. For the first time in a while I think maybe there's not really a problem between us. Maybe the whole boyfriend thing with Twig is gonna work out OK.

'Anyway, Magnus is right about the name,' Megan says, and Magnus looks chuffed. 'How about Sassy and the . . . Oh, I don't know – Sassy and the . . . errr . . . somethings?'

'Sassy and the Seagulls!' Sindi-Sue exclaims – and we all groan.

'We might end up sounding like seagulls,' Beano says drily. 'Let's not plant the idea in the audience's heads!'

'Sassy and the Sausages!' says Pip, who's just danced in to get the phone back.

'I don't think so,' I say as she pirouettes out. 'Not unless they're veggie!'

'Well, how about Sassy and the Wilde Bunch?' Beano suggests.

'That's it!' Magnus grins.

'Sounds cool to me,' Twig says and everyone else agrees.

'OK!' Cordelia runs her eye down the checklist. 'That's everything. All we need now is a bit of luck. So I'll put myself down to take care of that. Let me see, one medium-sized spell should do it.'

And she narrows her green eyes mischievously.

26

It's almost nine now and everyone's gone home. I'm sitting cross-legged on the floor, strumming my guitar, thinking how cool – and weird – it is that I've suddenly got such a big circle of friends and so many of them are boys. I mean, if anyone had said to me a few months ago that I'd be happy to have chicos like Beano and Magnus in my house, never mind my *room*, I would've thought they were crazy. But I suppose my life has changed in a whole lot of ways recently.

Then as I strum, *STRUM STRUM STRUM*, I think how exciting it is to be doing the concert, but how I mustn't forget *why* we're doing it, and my mind drifts to Taslima and Aisya and all the people caught up in the earthquake, *STRUM STRUM STRUM*, until a melody, then a few lines for a new song swim into my brain.

They were sleeping, they were dreaming
That the world would always be the same.

They were sleeping, they were dreaming
When the storms and the earthquakes came . . .

But I don't get any further, cos just then my mobile
starts ringing. I grab it from the bedside table and
check the caller ID.

The mobile continues to ring in my hand while
my brain turns into a boxing ring with two separate
bits of me slugging it out.

IMPETUOUS ME – in the red corner,
complete with boxing gloves and helmet and a
scarlet dress – wants me to answer right away! Cos
it's Phoenix and it loves the thrill it gets when it
hears his voice.

But LOYAL ME – in the white corner, complete
with soft white flowing dress, glittery angel wings
and luminescent halo – says *No! You are officially
Twig's girlfriend, Sassy. You shouldn't be having phone
conversations with any other chico.*

The mobile's still ringing. And before LOYAL
ME can stop her, IMPETUOUS ME whips off
her boxing glove and presses Answer.

'Hey, Sassy!' Phoenix's voice mainlines into my
ear. (IMPETUOUS ME punches the air triumphantly. LOYAL ME sulks.) 'Got you at last! I
thought you were never going to answer. So how
are things?'

'G-great,' I stammer as I try not to let my
increased heart rate make me sound like Brewster

after he's chased next-door's cat. Then my brain disconnects from my tongue and I'm off! 'Actually-I'm-going-to-be-singing-next-Saturday. Me-and-some-friends-are-getting-a-band-together. Just-a-teensy-gig-in-the-town-hall –'

'That's great news!' Phoenix interrupts, which is just as well cos I'm at serious risk of hyperventilation! 'You know, I was worried you wouldn't sing again after that recording deal knock-back. But you have to, Sassy. Singing's like breathing for people like us. We can't live without it.'

The way Phoenix says *'people like us'* makes my heart stop in its tracks. So much so that suddenly I can't speak at all. And neither does Phoenix. And in that silence something invisible, something magical seems to happen between us.

'I wish I could make your concert,' he says at last and IMPETUOUS ME swoons. 'I'm going to New York for my first ever US tour Sunday week. But listen, I was thinking, when I get back . . . maybe we could meet up?'

IMPETUOUS ME wants to shout *YES!* into the phone, but LOYAL ME clamps her hand over IMPETUOUS ME'S mouth.

'Sassy, are you still there?' Phoenix asks.

'Yeah, yeah, sure,' I stammer. 'Meet up? Yeah, that would be great.' IMPETUOUS ME does a victory lap of my brain while LOYAL ME slumps off miserably into the corner, her halo drooping.

Then we chat about what fun it was at the Wiccaman festival and how awful it must be for Taslima in the earthquake zone.

'OK,' he says after a while. 'I'll have to go now. Have a good one next Saturday.'

I say 'I'll try', I say 'Thanks for phoning', I say 'Bye'.

Then I lie back on my bed and stare at the ceiling, my brain churning round and round, all my thoughts in a tangle like tights in a washing machine. Thoughts about Twig and Phoenix and whether I should have told Phoenix I couldn't meet up with him ever. Or whether I should tell Twig I don't think the whole boyfriend/girlfriend thing is really working for me.

But as I get ready for bed I realize it's not just Twig and Phoenix I'm confused about. It's me . . . Cos sometimes it feels like I'm not just one person – but two, or even three different people, all at the same time. I stare at my reflection in the bathroom mirror, as if I might be able to see who I really am.

I wonder if Tas would say that being confused about yourself is all part of growing up. All part of being thirteen. All part of changing from the little girl I was to the woman[26] I'm going to be.

Or maybe she'd say that feeling like I'm three different people all at once is a sure sign of insanity!

[26] Aaargh! Freaky thought!

I wander back through to The Pig Pen, get into bed and pull the duvet up round my ears. And with thoughts of Phoenix and Twig and Tas and IMPETUOUS ME and LOYAL ME and even MIXED-UP ME all swirling round and round in my brain, I drift into a hot and troubled sleep . . .

. . . and into the weirdest dream.

I'm in Fossil Grove Old Folks' Home. I mean IN it, LIVING in it. I'm very old and very sad and the nurse has ordered me to go to see the resident psychologist.

I take my little-old-lady walking frame and totter through to a room with PSYCHOLOGIST on the door. Inside there's a desk, a couch and a big weeping fig plant. A woman in a white coat stands by the window, her back to me.

I gasp as she turns.

'Maybe you remember me?' she says. 'Taslima Ankhar – Dr Taslima Ankhar. We were at school together. I've been told you're having a problem with your depression. Would you like me to help you up on to the couch?'

Tas helps me up and I lie back. She goes to her computer and presses a few buttons. 'Just getting your files.' She stares at the screen as it clicks and whirrs. 'OK, so here's your life so far. You met your husband, Twig, when you were thirteen,' she reads. 'You lived with him for the next fifty years, then he disappeared in the Amazonian Rainforest, trying to stop them killing the last Hairy-legged Slime Toad in the world. You've been in Fossil Grove Old Folks' Home for the past two years, and you have suspected depression. Is that right?'

I stare at Taslima. MARRIED TO TWIG FOR FIFTY YEARS!

'I d-don't know, Doctor,' I stammer. 'I- I can't remember.'

Taslima smiles. 'It's all here on your file, so it must be true. You must have loved him very much.'

'But no,' I gasp. 'That is . . . I'm not sure.'

Taslima's eyes shoot up under her fringe. 'So, you're not sure? Well, let me ask you this – if you could turn time back, if you could have your life again, would you do anything different?' She whips out a notebook and pen, just like she used to when we were best buds at school.

I close my eyes and try to think. 'That's the thing,' I say at last. 'I really don't know..'

When Tas doesn't say anything I open my eyes. But she's gone. The weeping fig has gone. And I'm not on the psychologist's couch, I'm in my bed and the alarm is ringing.

Ringing, ringing, ringing.

27

Holy Guacamole! I must have drifted back to sleep after my scary dream, and when I wake again it's half nine, which means it's gonna be a mad rush to get to Megan's garage for our very first rehearsal at ten.

I leap from my bed, pull on a T-shirt and a pair of shorts, sling my guitar over my shoulder, grab a glass of fruit juice and a banana, and dash out. When I get to Megan's she's already at the back of the garage, dusting down her dad's drum kit. Twig's unravelling an extension cable and setting up a mike and some amplifiers. (Thank goodness he's busy, cos I still feel a bit confused about the phone call from Phoenix last night, not to mention the dream.) Cordelia's relaxing on a sun lounger, looking all witchy in a little black dress, her hair for once not tied up at all. Sindi-Sue's perched on a stool and Beano's not turned up yet.

'I'll be a fan, OK?' Sindi-Sue grins with a flick of her long blonde hair. 'I like being a fan!'

'And I'll be an impartial observer,' Cordelia says, playing with a spider she's found on the floor of the garage.

'Oh, and Magnus phoned to say he's already emailed the poster for the gig to us all,' Megan announces – as if it is the most natural thing in the world for Magnus to call her!

'I thought you had a problem with Magnus!' Cordelia shouts above the din of Megan fixing the cymbals on her drum kit.

'Yeah, after my party that time, I did.' She silences them with her hand. 'But he's changed quite a lot since then. He walked all the way home with me and Twig last night. He's really much more mature now.'

'OK,' says Twig, plugging a lead into his fiddle and pushing his flop of hair back. 'We can't wait forever for Beano. Maybe we should get started. If we can't make it work with the three of us, Beano's not gonna make a huge difference.'

So I get my guitar out and tune it up and minutes later I'm singing 'Why can't people be more like dolphins?' Tentatively, Megan adds in some drums at the back. Then Twig joins in. But even though it's obvious that Twig's a whizz on the fiddle, we find it hard to keep together and have to stop and start lots.

'I know, like, I'm not the most musical person on the planet,' Sindi-Sue says as we straggle to a halt. 'But maybe it would help if you all just played really LOUD!'

'Yeah,' Megan batters her drums. 'Isn't that what the first punk bands did? My dad said half of them didn't even know how to play their instruments. They just belted the songs out any old way!'

'I don't know,' I sigh. 'If people are paying to come and see us, we'll have to be a bit better than that. I think we need a lead guitarist to keep us all together.'

'Looks like we've got one,' Twig says as a car drives up and Beano gets out. 'Let's hope he can actually play the thing.'

We watch as Beano pulls a guitar and an amplifier from the boot, then waves as his mum drives off.

'How's it going?' he asks as he sets his stuff up.

'Emmm . . . The truth? Not brilliantly, mate,' Twig adjusts his bow. 'We've just tried one song all the way through.'

'And it was awful,' Megan says dismally.

'Aw, come on!' Sindi-Sue protests. 'It wasn't that bad.'

Suddenly, the whole futility of what we're trying to do hits me. 'Actually, it was. I guess it was a mad idea. I don't think we can do it.'

'Hey!' Beano protests as he looks around for a socket to plug his amp in. 'You're not even prepared to give me a chance? See what I can do?'

'Sorry,' I apologize. 'I didn't mean it that way.'

'Let Beano set up,' Twig says encouragingly, 'then we'll try the dolphin song again. I think if we work at it we can make a half-decent sound.'

So Beano gets tuned up. I strum a few times to take us into the song. Twig comes in on his fiddle and Megan adds the drums. We struggle all the way to the end of the second verse, better than before – but Beano hasn't played at all. Besides, he looks way too relaxed.

As we do the lead into the third verse, Twig and Megan exchange a look, and I guess they're thinking what I'm thinking. That Beano can't actually play. It would be typical. So many boys get a fancy lead guitar and then they pose in front of their bedroom mirrors, play a couple of chords and think that's all there is to it.

Then suddenly he's playing along, his long brown fingers quick and nimble. And the sound he's producing isn't just OK, it's fantastic!

When at last we reach the end, Sindi-Sue and Cordelia whoop and clap.

'Wow, man. You really know how to play that thing,' Twig says, impressed.

'Been playing since I was six,' Beano smiles his quiet smile.

'Yeah, and we've been in the same class since we were five, so how come I never knew?' I ask, curious as to how he'd never said, when he knew I was so into singing.

'I guess I just never thought to mention it.' Beano smiles shyly and flexes his fingers.

'OK, you guys!' Cordelia interrupts. 'Back to work. You've got a gig on Saturday and an hour's worth of songs to get together. You don't have time to relax.'

'Who wants to relax?' I strum my guitar. *STRUM STRUM STRUM*. 'This is rock 'n' roll, baby. Let's do it!'

28

Saturday. The day of the gig! And I am SO wound up. Last weekend we each emailed everyone on our contact lists. Magnus calls it grandly his 'viral marketing campaign'. He's right into all that kind of stuff. Actually, on impulse, I emailed everyone on Dad's list too, so who knows, maybe the Prime Minister got one! All week folk have emailed or texted back or said at school they'll be there.

On Monday, while the rest of us were at school, Twig took posters round the health centre and the library and the local shops and sweet-talked them into putting them up right away.

And when we told Miss Peabody about the benefit gig she let Megan and Magnus out to stick posters up all round the school. Magnus even persuaded Smollett to make an announcement over the school tannoy system!

'I think old Smollett's going senile,' Sindi-Sue giggled. 'His judgement's obviously impaired.'

'More like he didn't want to say no to Magnus,'

Megan said, all dreamy-eyed. 'After all, he is a star pupil.'

Cordelia looked like she was gonna vomit on the spot!

At lunchtime on Tuesday, a rumour went round that there was someone balanced on a ledge right at the top of the school clock tower. The whole school rushed out to the playing fields, thinking it was a suicidal teacher or something, and – guess what? – it was Mad Midge Murphy!

'What on *earth* are you doing, boy?' Smollett roared up at him.

'Putting up a poster for the charity gig, Sir,' Midge shouted back with a cheeky grin. 'For the benefit of low-flying aircraft.'

On Wednesday, Magnus checked out the hall while the rest of us were rehearsing.

'It's great,' he reported back. 'There's a lighting rig and a state-of-the-art sound system. Plus I got talking to the techie guy, Stefan. Seeing as it's a charity gig, Stefan says he'll do the sound and lights for us for nothing.'

On Thursday after school, Cordelia got a phone call from Taslima. She rushed round to let me know before I went out for band practice. Aisya is out of hospital now and Tas and her mum are making plans to come home. I was so relieved I almost burst into tears.

Of course, seeing Twig every day and not

knowing exactly how I feel about him has been weird . . . Most of the time I tried to ignore it cos there was a crowd of us there anyway, but each night, when it got close to the end of the practice, I felt pretty mixed up. A bit of me wanted him to walk me home, hoped that he'd take my hand, that he'd say sweet and lovely things to me, make me feel like what we have together is something really special, something more than just being buds. The other bit of me wasn't so sure.

There was also the fact that Magnus walked home with us cos he has to go past the end of my street, so it's not like a romantic walk home was really possible with him hanging around. Still, I couldn't help but notice that Twig wasn't in the least bothered. Magnus and him just nattered about the set-up for the stage on Saturday, like I wasn't even there.

At least the rehearsals have gone better than we expected. This morning we worked out a playlist of about an hour's worth of songs. We're gonna start with 'My Imaginary Friend's Not Sweet', then keep the tempo up with songs like 'Why Can't People Be More Like Dolphins', 'I Don't Want to be a Juliet to Your Romeo' and 'Sweatshop Kid'. In the middle set I'll do 'Jelly Baby Blues' and 'Bungee-jumping Heart' on my own with acoustic guitar. Then we'll do 'Pinch Me, I Think I Must Be Dreaming', 'If You Were a Panda', 'When the

Little Birds Stopped Singing' and 'Don't Put That Axe To My Throat' together. We'll finish on 'They Were Sleeping, They Were Dreaming', the song I wrote about the earthquake.

As we pack up our stuff at the end of our last rehearsal early on Saturday afternoon, Magnus gives us a pep talk like he's a football manager and we're his team! 'Don't worry tonight if it doesn't all sound polished,' he says. 'Everyone thinks it's great you're doing this to raise money for the earthquake. Nobody's expecting you to sound perfect.'

'Just as well,' Megan says, and everyone bursts out laughing.

I laugh too, but despite myself a little worry worm has burrowed its way into my consciousness. I mean, no one except me has ever been up on stage before. It's one thing playing to your mates in a garage; it's totally different getting up in front of a crowd – and we all need to come through to make it work. I just hope no one bottles it.

29

As soon as I get in Mum nabs me and absolutely insists I lie down in my room for a while. 'If you don't calm down, you'll end up too exhausted to climb up on to the stage tonight, never mind sing.'

'Yeah, you'll burn out like Arizona Kelly and have to go off to a rehab clinic and get therapy and stuff,' Pip says solemnly as she feeds a strip of carrot peel to Mrs Houdini. 'Then I'll make a fortune selling my story to the papers. "MY LIFE OF HELL WITH MY PSYCHO BIG SIS".'

'Well, work out another way to make your fortune, little sis,' I say, grabbing a wooden spoon and singing into it like it's a mike. 'Cos Miss Sassy Wilde is on top of her game and she ain't gonna burn out.'

'Sassy!' Mum interrupts. 'Go to your room NOW, or I'm going to take you to Great-Gran's to calm you down.'

'No way!' I squeal, waving a pair of Pip's pants[27] as a surrender flag and retreating upstairs. (Thing is, I love my great-gran, but she is SO strict. She still believes that little girls should be seen and not heard. Visiting her has been known to induce a state similar to catatonia. ZZZzzzZZZzzzZZZZ!)

It's five o'clock – and I may have been in my room for a while but I can't say I've calmed down. I mean, there are so many things to worry about.

The Wilde Bunch is scheduled to meet at the hall at 18.30 hours. Magnus has copied out a precise timetable for us all, planning it like a military operation. Megan thinks he has wonderful organizational skills, but I suspect he's a control freak.

I've booked Pip to do some corkscrew-curl magic on my hair at half past five. Dad's offered to give me a lift to the town hall, but with all the electricity Pip's going to be using to transform my hair, as well as the amplifiers and lights at the benefit gig, I reckon I've used up my carbon allowance for the week, so I insist I'll be fine walking.

I try lying down, but I really can't. I'm far too hyped up, so I'm flicking through the clothes in my wardrobe, wondering what to wear, when my hand

[27] Most of Pip's pants are coloured: sizzling pink, wicked red, luminous lime. This is Pip's ONLY white pair. And very frilly!

brushes Phoenix's shirt and I get this weird sensation, almost like an electric shock. I take the shirt out and sit on the edge of the bed, holding it, thinking about Phoenix and how much I like it when he calls. It's strange to think too that Sindi-Sue dreams about marrying Phoenix. That Megan likes to sleep with his poster above her bed. I smile to myself. For hundreds of girls, I suppose, Phoenix *is* a dream boyfriend. And OK, he texts me once in a while, but he's going off to the States soon. He's going to be a big star one day. He's bound to forget about the girl who sang with him at the Wiccaman festival.

Just then the grandfather clock in the hall chimes. If I don't get a move on I'll be late! Quickly, I hang the dream boyfriend's shirt on its hanger and shove it to the back of the wardrobe, then I shut my eyes and pull something out at random. Yay! It's my oversized 'Save the Siberian Tiger' T-shirt. Good choice! I pull it on and jump into a pair of black leggings and I'm about to stick my feet into my fave Birkenstocks when Pip pokes her head round the door.

'Miss Pip, beautician and hairdresser to the stars is ready for you now!' she announces. I follow her through to The Pink Palace where she's got the tongs all heated up in front of a make-up mirror with lights all round it. Expertly, Pip twists my hair into a mass of glossy corkscrew curls. Then it's a

touch of glimmer on the eyes, mascara on the lashes, a smidgeon of gloss on the lips –

'Presenting Miss Sassy Wilde!' I announce grandly, throwing my arms wide and twirling a few times when she's finished. 'What do you think, Princess Pip?'

Pip purses her lips. 'Mmm . . . I suppose you'll do,' she says at last. 'Personally, I prefer pink. And dresses. And maybe a tiara?'

'Well, I think I look great, little sis. Thanks a million!' I hug her till she squeaks, then dash back to my own room, grab my guitar, clatter downstairs two-at-a-time, leap over Brewster, shout *Bye-eee everyone, see you there*!' and rocket out the door – THIS IS IT!!

As I approach the town hall, zillions of worry worms hatch in my tummy, all wriggling, squirming and squiggling as all the worst-case scenarios crowd my head:

1. Beano gets stage fright and won't play
2. Megan throws a wobbly and storms off
3. Twig just doesn't turn up
4. The audience doesn't turn up
5. I lose my voice
6. I don't lose my voice, but I sing totally out of tune like Sindi-Sue, and everyone boos me and throws things.

For an awful moment I think I'm gonna have a total panic attack, then someone will find me hyperventilating on the pavement, grasping my chest, and think I'm having a heart attack and call an ambulance. Next thing I'll be lying in hospital with an oxygen mask on, protesting 'I'm fine – you've got to let me go, I've got a gig to do at the town hall.' And they'll think I'm hallucinating and send me to a mental-institution-type-place and I'll never ever get out again!

Just in time I remember the calming-down advice Taslima gave me yonks ago – 'Breathe through your heels.'[28]

So that's what I do. And as I climb the steps to the big main doors of the town hall, the heel-breathing starts to work its magic and my tummy settles and my breathing returns to normal. Wey-hey!

The hall looks great! There's a low stage with big loudspeakers either side, and a dance floor in front; then further back – cos it's pretty huge – there are little round tables and chairs.

Cordelia arrives right after me. She looks gorgeous and otherworldly in a rainbow frou-frou skirt dotted with tiny silver stars. On her feet she's wearing silver ankle-strap sandals, and instead of tying her hair up with ribbons, she's used silver tinsel. It sparkles stunningly against the jet black

[28] Don't knock it until you try it – it works!

of her hair. To finish the look she's brushed her eyelids and cheekbones with pale blue glitter and wound strings of tiny crystal beads in pastel colours round her neck and wrists.

'It's my Fairy Goth look,' she says, twirling an imaginary wand.

'Good fairy or bad fairy?' Magnus, who's looking really cool in a black T-shirt and black jeans, asks.

'Good fairy, of course! I can make your dreams come true!' She smiles sweetly . . . before adding mischievously. 'Unless, of course, you annoy me!'

Just then the hall doors burst open and Megan clatters in, hauling various bits of drum kit. Magnus immediately rushes over to help and for a moment they stand grinning at each other like half-witted Cheshire cats. Cordelia and me exchange a look.

'Are you thinking what I'm thinking?' Cordelia giggles.

'I guess I am,' I smile.

Magnus is carrying the drums now, and Megan's tossing her hair and laughing – and it is SO OBVI-OUS that they fancy each other!

'Actually, I think they look sweet together,' Cordelia sighs.

And they do. It's like they're both glowing in a golden bubble and everything outside of them has ceased to exist.

And though I'm happy for Megan and Magnus, I feel sad for me. Cos that's what it *should* be like.

And the truth is, it's not like that with me and Twig. Not any more.

Cordelia turns and stares at me like she's reading my thoughts. 'You're gonna have to tell him,' she says quietly.

'What? Who? What d'you mean?' I bluster.

'Twig. You're not into him any more. There's no point in putting it off.' Cordelia holds my gaze and I know there's no point in lying to her, of all people.

'OK, I know I should. I've known for a while,' I sigh. 'The thing is, I don't know if I can . . . Twig's so sweet. I don't want to hurt him.'

Just then Beano shouts from the stage. 'Hey, Sassy! Stefan's ready to do your sound check!'

With a heavy heart I hurry up onstage, strap my guitar on and tune it up. *Twang. Twa-a-a-ng. Twang.*

Moments later, Twig arrives. He takes out his shiny blue electric fiddle, smoothes his bow and smiles at me through his flop of hair. And even though I want there to be, in that moment I know for sure. The magic between us has gone. I don't understand why, and maybe I never will, but over the past few weeks something has changed between us.

Cordelia's right, I think miserably as I adjust the height of the mike, *I do have to tell him.* But now's not the time. Whatever's gonna happen between me and Twig will have to wait till after the gig.

30

While we've been doing the sound check and Magnus has been staring all dewy-eyed at Megan, Cordelia and Sindi-Sue have been busy setting up a system for collecting the money.

'We've put a row of buckets with *Earthquake Appeal Fund* labels on a table by the entrance,' Sindi-Sue explains as I stop on my way to the dressing room that Stefan's told us the band can use. 'We're gonna ask people to donate at least two quid as they come in.'

'And if they even think about not putting something in –' Cordelia says, her eyes glittering, – 'they'll be sorry.'

In the dressing room I check my make-up one last time. Thankfully, it's OK. Not a smudge of mascara anywhere it shouldn't be, though I figure there's not even a trace of gloss left on my lips. And I'm on my way back to the hall when Twig appears at the far end of the deserted corridor, obviously heading for the dressing room too.

I can't help but think how gorgeous he looks. And I wonder if I really do want to split up with him. I mean, he's always been so sweet with me. He never gets angry or moody or huffy. And he gets on so well with Pip. Even Brewster adores him. Maybe I'm expecting too much from having a boyfriend. Maybe you can only have that magic thing at the start of a relationship. Thing is, me and Twig have been together for a couple of weeks now. Maybe it's not realistic to expect the romance to stay. Maybe if I tried a bit harder I could make things work out.

Twig's almost level with me now. He smiles kinda shyly through his flop of hair. And I don't mean to. I really don't. But before I can stop myself, I'm blurting, 'Twig-I'm-sorry-I-don't know-the-right-way-to-do-this-and-maybe-this-isn't-the-right-time-and-it's-not-that-I-don't-think-you're-great-cos-I-do-it's-just-I . . . I . . . I don't think I can be your girlfriend any more.'

I clamp my hand to my mouth. Too late. The words are out now. Hanging in the air between us, like tiny bombs detonating.

Twig stares at me, his tanned face suddenly pale. And I feel so awful. Like a hunter who's just pounced on a totally innocent baby seal and bludgeoned it with a great big emotional club it didn't see coming.

Instantly, I want to undo it. 'I'm sorry. I shouldn't have said that. I'm just confused . . .' I gabble, tears springing up in my eyes. 'It's probably nerves, you know, with the pressure . . .'

'No, no, it's OK.' He runs his hand through his hair. 'I've been thinking about things too . . . Remember that time we were walking home – well, I was on my skateboard – and you asked why didn't I go to school? Do you remember what I said?'

'Yeah, you said you were a free spirit . . .' I mumble miserably. 'And you caught a butterfly, and you said that if you went to school it would be like putting it in a jar . . .'

'Well, that's the thing,' Twig's voice is soft. 'I didn't want to hurt you either, so I couldn't say anything. But this whole boyfriend thing . . . it's been making me feel kinda hemmed in, kinda pinned down . . . I mean, I love hanging out with you, having fun and everything . . . and I think you're great. But really, I've been wanting to tell you for a while. I'd rather we were just friends.'

I take a huge breath and fall back against the wall. 'You have no idea what a relief that is!' I gasp, drying a tear from the corner of my eye. 'I was terrified I was gonna hurt you –'

'Relax,' Twig says softly. 'I'm not hurt at all.' Then he reaches his hand out, gently touches my hair and looks deep into my eyes. 'You'll always be special to me, Sassy Wilde. You'll always be my first girlfriend. The first girl I ever kissed.'

And when he says that, something in my heart twangs, ever so softly.

31

Back in the hall, Beano's lounging on a chair, looking totally cool.

'Aren't you nervous?' I ask, amazed.

Beano shakes his head. 'Nah, I'm pretending
I'm Jimi Hendrix, my all-time hero. He wouldn't
be nervous, would he?'

'Hardly,' Megan giggles, fiddling with a plaster
on her blistered finger. 'He's dead.'

Just then Magnus shouts from the stage. 'Hey,
Sassy and the Wilde Bunch! Stefan says would you
like to do a song all the way through to settle your
nerves before we open the doors?'

'That's not a bad idea.' Beano stretches like a
sleek black cat. 'Not, of course, that I have any
nerves to settle.'

'How about "My Imaginary Friend's Not
Sweet"?' Twig suggests as we make our way up
on to the stage. 'It's funny and fast and it's what
we're planning to open with, so it'll get us in the
mood.'

Moments later we're all set. Megan starts battering into the drums, then me and Beano join in with the guitars and I belt out the first lines:

My imaginary friend's not sweet —
She's big and she's mean
And she's got giant feet.

Twig grins at me as he comes in with his fiddle, and I fly into the second verse.

My imaginary friend's real fierce.
Gonna pick on me? Gonna push me around?
Gonna name-call or tease?
Then you'd better think twice
Cos she's really not nice . . .

Megan batters the drums ferociously and clashes the cymbals, then we all blast out together so by the time we finish we're totally buzzed up and every nerve in my body is zinging.

'OK, folks! It's quarter past seven. Time to open the doors, let the public in,' Stefan announces over the loudspeakers. 'Everyone ready?'

'Group hug!' Sindi-Sue squeals, throwing her arms round a startled Twig. Laughing, we all join in.

'This is it!' I whoop. 'Let's do it for Taslima!'

When Stefan opens the main doors we do a double take. There's a huge queue of people! Tons of kids from our year stream in, all in their party gear. And lots of seniors. And kids I've never seen before. I even see Miss Cassidy coming in, looking fab in a funky black dress with a zingy pink sash. And she's not alone! She's with a dark-haired man I think must be her boyfriend. And he's totally eye-meltingly, toe-curlingly GORGEOUS.

I'm busy waving 'HI!' to people, when Mum's hippy friend Cathy struggles through the swing doors with a huge box. Twig rushes over to take it from her before she drops it.

'It's lemonade to keep you all hydrated,' Cathy explains, pushing back a few strands of hair from her glistening brow. 'There's another couple of crates to come in from the camper.' Midge and Magnus dash out to get the rest of the boxes, while Cathy commandeers a table at the back of the hall. 'I'll put a couple of bowls out for donations,' Cathy smiles. 'Any money collected can go towards the benefit fund.'

'Thanks, Cathy,' I beam and give her a big hug.

'*Nullo problemo, chica*,' Cathy laughs as she busies herself with setting out bottles and cans and recyclable paper cups. 'What you and your buddies are doing is great. Love and peace is all very well, sweetie, but people in crisis need hard dosh too.'

Tons more people arrive while Cathy's getting her juice bar set up, including Miss Peabody and

Mr Hemphead, who retreat towards the relative quiet of the chairs at the back.

Then Karim Malik arrives with his dad who runs the Indian restaurant, The Wee Curry House, in the town centre.

'Karim told me all about what his classmates were doing,' Mr Malik says. 'So I wanted to donate something too.' He waves his hand and four waiters come hurrying over laden with take-away boxes.

I stare in wonder as Stefan sets up more tables at the side of the hall and the waiters arrange dozens of dishes filled with pakoras, samosas, bhajis and poppadums.

'Just in case you all get a bit peckish,' Mr Malik grins.

'This is so exciting!' Sindi-Sue squeals. 'We've got everything we need now for a fab party!'

'Yeah, we've got everything all right,' I exclaim ruefully as Mum and Dad come in with a pink Princess Pip in a prom dress and flashing-light tiara. 'We've even got my parentals!' And everyone laughs.

Every time another clump of people arrives Sindi-Sue wiggles over, flapping her hands and squealing, 'Hi! So glad you could come!' while Cordelia stands by the row of collection buckets, making sure everyone puts something in. All I have to worry about now is whether or not Sassy and the Wilde Bunch can actually hold it together for an hour!

As I skirt down the side of the hall to get to the stage, Pip comes rushing over in a swish of taffeta, her face shining. I'm sure she's got lipgloss and mascara on, and are those false eyelashes?! But even worse – she's got three boys in tow.

'This is my big sister, Sassy,' she tells the boys, who gaze at her adoringly. 'She's gonna be a star.'

I make a mental note to tell Pip three things later.

A. I'm not gonna be a star.
B. She is far too young to have a boyfriend – let alone three!
C. Being single is a wonderful thing. I am the living proof of that – I feel so much better being on my own!

32

Up on stage I look out over the crowds of excited people spilling about the hall and my tummy lurches dangerously. I honestly never thought that so many people would come. And the more there are, the less sure I am that we can actually pull this off.

Nervously, I take my guitar from its stand and loop the strap over my shoulder. Twig picks up his fiddle, Beano straps on his guitar and Megan settles in behind her drums. Stefan gives us a thumbs-up and turns the hall lights down. Slowly, the crowd falls silent. For a split second there's total darkness. Then the stage floods with swirling blues and pinks and reds, Megan lifts her sticks to start the drum intro, and we're about to launch into the first number – when there's a kerfuffle at the back of the hall.

Megan hesitates – unsure whether or not to start, when suddenly the hall lights flicker on once more. Everyone turns and stares as the doors at the back burst open – and a silver-haired lady zooms in on a motorized scooter. She's got brightly coloured balloons tied to her handlebars printed with *HAPPY BIRTHDAY, PEGGY! 100 TODAY!* Instantly, I recognize her. It's the elderly lady from Fossil Grove Old Folks' Home, the one who told me I shouldn't give up singing. And she's followed by a whole gang of old people! Some with walking frames, some walking arm in arm, some in wheelchairs, some pushing wheelchairs, all babbling excitedly.

'We'll just be a minute!' shouts a man in a tweed jacket. 'That darned Mrs Pratchett! Would've been easier getting out of Colditz!'

Peggy peeps the horn on her motorized scooter and the crowds of young people part to let her through. She comes to a halt in front of the stage and beams up at me.

'We're delighted you decided to sing again, Sassy,' she says, her blue eyes sparkling. 'And we're sorry we're late. We wouldn't have missed this for the world.' Then she turns and scoots off to the back of the hall.

Minutes later everyone's settled, the hall lights flicker off, the stage lights buzz on once more in a blaze of dancing, swirling colour and . . .

BA-BA-BA-BA-BA-BOOM! Megan hits the drums, Beano's guitar squeals into life, and I blast into the first verse of 'My Imaginary Friend's Not Sweet.'

Then we hit the chorus and Twig swings his fiddle up under his chin and lets rip. All the way through we keep it together and when we get to the end the audience applauds enthusiastically.

Over the next couple of numbers we get more confident. Every so often one of us hits a duff note, or Megan doesn't get the beat quite right, but we just ride over it.

Then I'm into my two solo numbers and Stefan puts the spotlight on me. Halfway through 'Jelly Baby Blues' my voice suddenly wobbles, but I quickly recover and at the end there's a big burst of applause.

Feeling really good about the way things are going I glance at the next song on the playlist. My heart thumps against my ribs. Cos it's 'Pinch Me, I Think I Must Be Dreaming', the song I wrote especially for Twig when I really thought, you know, that he was The One.

I'm supposed to play the opening chords to lead Beano and the others in. But panic grips me. Cos I'm not sure I can ever sing that song again, not now me and Twig aren't together any more. I glance anxiously over my shoulder. Beano's poised, waiting for me to start. Megan's at the ready with her drums. The crowd grows restless.

And I'm still dithering, when Twig steps over beside me, swings his fiddle up under his chin and plays the intro. I look at him, surprised, and he smiles encouragingly. Then I'm singing and Twig's playing and it's the loveliest and the saddest feeling all at once, cos my voice and the fiddle seem to blend into a perfect harmony and I guess everyone listening thinks we're hopelessly, crazily, soppily in love – but me and Twig both know we're not.

When we get to the end there's a thunderclap of applause.

'You know, it will always be your song,' I whisper to Twig, a big lump in my throat. And it's all I can do not to burst into tears.

Then someone passes me a note up on stage. I read it quickly. Of course! I should have thought. 'This next song's for a very special lady,' I say into the mike, my voice steadying. 'A lady who's a hundred years old today.' I pause as everyone cheers. 'A lady called Peggy, who gave me a piece of advice I'll never forget.'

Then I start up, 'Happy Birthday to you! Happy Birthday to you!' Beano joins in, making his guitar really sing the melody, just like his hero Jimi Hendrix did with 'The Star-Spangled Banner' at the end of Woodstock[29]. Peggy's friends push her into the middle of the hall on her scooter and soon there's a big circle round her and everyone's singing 'Happy Birthday' and Peggy's old face is totally glowing.

We move straight into 'If You Were a Panda', then follow it up as planned with 'When the Little Birds Stopped Singing' and the fast and

[29] The first ever big summer music festival in 1969. Can you believe it, Mum's friend Cathy was actually THERE!

furious 'Don't Put That Axe To My Throat'.

Beano's halfway through a guitar solo when I see Midge Murphy emerging from the crowd. Suddenly, he leaps right into the middle of the stage and starts weaving and bopping with the hottest dance moves imaginable.

The crowd roars with delight and then everyone's dancing, jumping up and down, waving their arms, swinging each other around, whooping. Midge does a double backflip and I grab my mike stand and move it away to make more room for him.

Then Twig goes manic on the fiddle and Megan crashes the cymbals. And the atmosphere is absolutely electric. It's like we're surfing on a huge wave of energy that's coming partly from us, partly from the crowd.

As Beano finishes with a wild screeching slide down the strings, Midge does an amazing head spin, then collapses in a crumpled, exhausted heap.

Totally hot and sweating and buzzing, we finally reach the last song on our playlist.

'This is our closing number,' I say into the mike, still trying to get my breath back. A few people shout things like, 'No, we want more!' and 'What about the encore?'

'I want to say thanks to all of you for coming. You've been a great crowd, and what's more, you've helped us raise money for all the people caught up in the earthquake. That means a lot to us, and to our friend Taslima, who's in Pakistan right now. And one last thing before we finish: I'd like to say thanks too to a fantastic band –' I turn and grin at Megan, Beano and Twig –'the Wilde Bunch. This is our first gig together, and I hope it won't be our last.'

There's a huge round of applause and everyone's whooping and hollering. I wait till the crowd falls quiet, then I take the mike from the stand, walk to the very front of the stage, and unaccompanied, I start to sing.

> They were sleeping, they were dreaming
> That the world would always be the same . . .

My voice echoes strong and clear, the crowd stands perfectly still, almost as if it's become one entity, holding its breath.

> They were sleeping, they were dreaming
> When the storm clouds and the earthquakes
>   came . . .

Quietly, Beano steps forward with his mike and takes up the next two lines:

> Cos none of us knows what fate has in store;
> None of us knows what's through the next door.

Megan steps forward now and sings:

So live each day like it might be the last.
Don't fret about the future, don't get hung up
on the past.

Then me, Beano and Megan sing together:

Cos it's NOW that matters, it's NOW that's
real
And have I told you lately . . . 'bout the way I
feel?
About you . . . about you . . . about you . . .

As our voices fade to a whisper, Twig comes gently in with a soulful fiddle riff. I gaze out over the sea of swaying, silent people, and as I do, I understand something. Something Twig saw when I was still blind to it.

That not getting a record deal with Y-Generation wasn't such a bad thing. That when I was getting excited about being a star, I was teetering on the edge of the slippery slope that ends up where Arizona Kelly is now, thinking it's about the fame, the celebrity, the platinum discs – thinking it's about ME.

When it's not about me at all. THIS is what it's about. Writing and singing songs that touch people, sharing those songs with people I love. Using my songs and my singing to help others.

And nothing and nobody will ever stop me doing that again.

33

When the applause eventually fades, I set my guitar on its stand and jump down from the stage. Instantly I'm mobbed by friends telling me how much they enjoyed themselves. Then the Fossil Grove old people push through to say they have to head back to the home and face the music with Mrs Pratchett.

'Great party!' they shout as they head towards the door. 'Thanks a million!'

'Matron has us on a curfew,' Peggy explains as she prepares to scoot off. 'Thanks for the music, Sassy. You must never let anyone stop you singing!'

'Don't worry, Peggy,' I smile, 'I'm not going to.'

'In that case, you're going to need a manager!' Magnus chips in excitedly as Peggy motors off. 'I've got some ideas, Sass. After all, we've made this concert work. This is just the beginning –'

'Aren't you forgetting something?' I interrupt, desperate to get a drink from Cathy's juice bar at the back of the hall before I totally dehydrate.

'I mean, I think it's great, everything you've done to make tonight work, but I've blown my chances of ever getting a recording deal, Magnus. I might be singing again, but without a recording deal, I'm going nowhere.'

'But that's the thing. You don't need a recording deal with anyone!' Magnus protests. 'We can release the band's first single online. You've already got a fan base, Sassy. Kids out there want your stuff. You've got a band. You don't need a recording company.'

Megan beams adoringly at him. 'I'm up for it,' she says. 'It was good playing drums again.'

'Sounds cool to me,' says Beano, tucking his plectrum through his guitar strings. 'Count me in.'

'Well, it'll have to wait,' I insist. 'Cos if I don't get a drink I might never sing again anyway.'

I leave the others excitedly discussing e-marketing and music downloads and head for Cathy's juice bar. With so many people milling about, wanting to tell me how great the gig's been, it takes me a while to struggle through to the back of the hall, by which time my tongue feels like it's grafted itself on to the roof of my mouth.

'Sorry, sweetie. All the juices were finished long ago,' Cathy apologizes. 'But if you're really desperate, and you don't mind my germs, you can have this.' She digs a bottle of water out of her shoulder bag.

Thankfully, I open it and tip my head back and start glugging so greedily it spills down my chin and dribbles down my T-shirt. I'm about to raise the bottle to my lips for a second time when I realize there's someone grinning at me from the shadows at the side of the hall. Someone with dark curly hair . . . and sparkling eyes . . . and the most beautiful smile.

I blink in amazement. After all, it might be a hallucination, mightn't it? A mirage, like you get in the desert. The result of extreme thirst and too much excitement.

While my brain works out that the chico now walking towards me is no mirage, no hallucination, my heart does a wild flamenco dance, all swirling scarlet skirts and stamping feet and clicking castanets.

'Hi,' Phoenix says as I wipe my dribbly chin with the back of my hand and try not to burp.

'Hi!' I say and my heart shouts *OLE!*

We stand grinning at each other for what seems like ages . . . when suddenly, Sindi-Sue rushes across the hall squawking, 'OMIGAWD! OMIGAWD! OMIGAWD!', her eyes so wide they look like they're going to totally POP and fall out on the floor.

'Phoenix, this is Sindi-Sue,' I laugh. 'I think she quite likes your music.'

Sindi-Sue's face is shining. 'I'm, like, your

number one fan ever,' she gasps. 'Will you marry me?'

''Fraid not,' Phoenix smiles. 'Would an autograph do instead?'

Sindi-Sue nods her head so much I worry she's gonna cause herself brain damage. Then Phoenix finds a pen and autographs the back of Sindi-Sue's hand and promises he'll send her a signed copy of his new CD and she babbles that she's never ever gonna wash her hand again and if ever he changes his mind about the marriage proposal, just to call and she'll be ready.

Which is when I notice Twig, his fiddle strapped over his shoulder, his skateboard under his arm, quietly slipping out of the door.

'Back in a minute!' I call to Phoenix.

By the time I reach the outside door, Twig's almost at the bottom of the steps.

'Twig!' I call. 'Hold on!'

He turns and looks up at me through his flop of hair. Suddenly, I don't know what to say. That is, my *heart* knows what it wants to say, but my *brain* doesn't know how to say it.

'Thanks,' I say at last.

'What for?' he smiles.

I walk slowly down the last few steps towards him. 'For everything . . . Listen, I didn't know Phoenix was coming. I mean it wasn't set up or anything . . . I just wanted you to know.'

'Don't worry, Sass,' he grins. 'It was a great gig. I had a ball. I've been blocked about performing in front of people for ages. I guess I'm not now –'

I gaze into his eyes, trying hard to see if he's really OK, or if he's just being incredibly generous-spirited and sweet.

'So . . . we're still friends?' I ask tentatively.

'I hope so.' He drops his skateboard to the pavement with a clatter. 'Gotta go,' he says. 'And I think there's someone waiting for you inside.'

Then he whizzes off, crazily weaving round the pavement bollards, shouting, 'Be wild, Sassy Wilde!'

And I stare after him, thinking, *What an amazing, wonderful, crazy chico!*

Back in the almost empty hall, Sindi-Sue has at last left Phoenix alone, but my heart sinks when I see who's cornered him now – Dad!

I rush over in time to hear Dad saying, 'We've got this super cycle safety gear we're trying to encourage youngsters to use. Maybe you could help us promote it?'

'Is this man being a nuisance?' I interrupt, grabbing Dad by the arm. 'Cos if he is I can call the police.'

'You'd best speak to my agent about the cycle campaign, Mr Wilde,' Phoenix says diplomatically, as Mum, who's also spotted what's happening, arrives and drags Dad away to collect the buckets of money from Cordelia.

'Listen, Sassy,' Phoenix says, when at last we're on our own. 'Ben's waiting outside for me. We're actually on our way to the airport. I leave for New York at midnight. You know, for the US tour.'

'Oh,' I say, disappointed.

The hall's deserted now. Cathy's taken her empty boxes out to the camper. Up on stage Stefan is winding up the cables for the mikes and putting them away. Mum and Dad and Pip are waiting by the door with the collection buckets.

'I'll just be a minute!' I shout to the parentals. 'I'll get you at the car!'

As Mum and Dad and Pip trail out, Phoenix comes up on to the stage with me to get my guitar.

'I caught most of the gig,' he says. 'You were great. Totally awesome. You know you can do this, Sassy. You're too good not to. And if there's any way I can help, all you have to do is ask.'

'Thanks,' I smile. 'I might just hold you to that!'

Outside it's dark now. A beautiful still night with stars twinkling and a big golden moon shining above the rooftops of Strathcarron. Ben's big black Hummer is parked just across the road. He gives a friendly wave and I wave back.

'I wouldn't have missed tonight for anything.' Phoenix says, and suddenly we're locked in a perfect golden bubble, floating up, up, up. 'And here, I brought this for you.' He hands me a CD. 'It's an advance copy.'

In the light from the streetlamp I read the title – and my heart melts and runs into my feet. '"Crazy Girl",' I say softly.

'I hope you don't mind. I kinda based the title track on you.'

I look into his eyes, dark-lashed and deep. His face is only centimetres from mine, and before I even really realize, like it's the most natural thing in the world, he's kissing me gently on the lips. Everything outside of us ceases to exist and the golden bubble soars higher and higher till it feels like I could reach out and touch the moon and gather a handful of stars from the sky. And I want the moment to last forever . . .

Then Dad drives up alongside us and Pip rolls down the window and shouts, 'Hey! Sassy! Are you ever coming home? I'm tired!'

The golden bubble bursts. But my heart stays up in the sky, twirling happily among the stars. Phoenix puts my guitar in the boot for me, then opens the car door and waits while I get in, like he doesn't really want me to go.

'Have a great time in New York,' I smile up at him as Dad revs the engine as if to say he wants to get going. 'Blow them away.'

'I'll do my best,' Phoenix holds my gaze for a magic moment longer. 'And I'll call you when I get a chance, OK?' Then he closes the door, Dad drives off, and I land back to earth with a thud.

34

On the way home exhaustion hits me hard as a fist. By the time we pull up in the drive I can hardly drag myself into the house.

I may be totally tired out, but I'm happy too. Tonight went so much better than any of us could have imagined, and though I don't know how much money we've collected, I do know the buckets are heavy. Very heavy.

Mum and Dad offer to count the money while I go for a shower.

By the time I get back to the kitchen, all squeaky clean in my Greenpeace nightie, the table's covered in little towers of pound coins and fifty-pence and twenty-pence pieces.

'Every tower is ten pounds,' Pip says excitedly, bopping about in a red lace negligee. 'And there are sixty-seven and a half towers!'

I'm no whizz at maths, and I'm supernaturally tired, but even so my brain click-click-clicks. 'Six hundred and seventy-five pounds!' I squeal.

'We've raised six hundred and seventy-five pounds!'

'People obviously put in more than two quid each,' Dad grins. 'Your mum had the brilliant idea of passing the buckets round at the end as people were leaving. I think they appreciated what a great gig you did –'

'It wasn't just me,' I say quickly. 'It would never have happened without everybody mucking in. But six hundred and seventy-five pounds! I can hardly believe we got that much. I can't wait to tell Tas!' Tears tweak at my eyes as I sink into a chair.

'But you didn't get six hundred and seventy-five pounds!' Pip exclaims. 'Look!' Excitedly, she waves a piece of pale blue paper in my face.

'What?' I grab the paper from Pip and stare at it, bemused. 'B-But how?' I stammer, shocked. Cos in my hand is a cheque for a thousand pounds!

'Look at the name.' Mum grins, pointing to the bottom right-hand corner.

'"Mrs Peggy Miller",' I read slowly, still not quite able to take it in.

'Peggy says you and your friends gave her the best birthday party she's *ever* had,' Mum explains, 'so she wanted to make a special donation to the benefit fund.'

Stunned, I stare at the towers of money, the thousand-pound cheque. But I don't see money. I see kindness and thoughtfulness and generosity. And I know it will help people whose homes have been destroyed in the earthquake – and mean so much to Taslima. Suddenly, I can't hold the tears back any more. They come streaming down my face.

'Oh dear, Sassy,' Mum says anxiously. 'What's wrong, honey?'

'Nothing,' I sob. 'I'm sorry . . . *sniff sniff* . . . I can't help it . . . *sniff sniff* . . . I'm just so happy!'

Yay! Guess where I am?

Taslima's house! For our Friday night sleepover.

On Wednesday when I got home from school, Taslima and Mrs Ankhar were sitting at the kitchen table with Mum. As soon as I walked in, Tas rushed over and hugged me really tight. 'We got back last night,' she explained, her hair lank, her eyes dark-shadowed. 'So we're a bit jet-lagged . . . but Mum wanted to speak to you as soon as possible.'

'What you've done is wonderful.' Mrs Ankhar said quietly, holding up a copy of the *Strathcarron Chronicle* with the headline *SASSY ROCKS STRATHCARRON FOR EARTHQUAKE APPEAL*. 'And this morning Taslima insisted I watch that clip of you at the Wiccaman festival again –'

'Yeah, with the sound up this time!' Taslima giggled.

'I owe you an apology, Sassy,' Mrs Ankhar said.

'I was wrong in thinking you might be a bad influence on Taslima. You're exactly the kind of girl she should be friends with.'

Tas invited Megan to tonight's sleepover too, cos after sleeping rough in Pakistan – sometimes with as many as ten people in one tent – Mrs Ankhar realized it's silly to be so strict about numbers. *Having good friends is what's important,* she says now, so she no longer has a no-more-than-two-friends-at-a-time sleepover party rule.

'It's a shame Megan couldn't come,' I say, as we tuck into some lovely treats Mrs Ankhar has made especially for us.

'I think it's great she's going to Sindi-Sue's for a Pink Pamper Pillow Party,' Taslima says thoughtfully. 'Sounds like they're best buds now.'

'Yeah, I think they are.' Cordelia lazily licks a blob of sticky icing from her fingers.

'I guess since I've been away Sindi-Sue's become part of our big friendship circle too,' Tas says happily.

'And Magnus and Beano and Twig,' Cordelia giggles. 'But I'm glad it's just the three of us tonight. Our special, magical friendship triangle.'

'I missed you so much when you weren't around, Tas,' I mumble through a mouthful of sweet samosa. 'And I was so worried about you. I was scared something awful might have happened –'

'OK!' Taslima says, leaping up. 'Enough of all this soppy emotional stuff. Time for a DVD! So what are we going to watch first? Cordelia's *Corpses on the Run* or my brand-new *Moonstruck in Mumbai?*'

'*Moonstruck in Mumbai!*' me and Cordelia shout, then we Bollywood dance round the room, wiggling our hips and twirling our wrists and making big romantic eyes at each other.

By the time we've watched both DVDs – and eaten all the delish treats – we're pretty sleepy so, as the final credits roll up on *Corpses on the Run*, Cordelia gropes for the remote control and flicks the DVD player and TV off.

'Sassy,' Taslima whispers into the darkness. 'Have you heard anything more from Phoenix?'

'Nah,' I say quietly as I snuggle deeper into my sleeping bag. 'I mean, he's lovely, and it was really sweet of him to come to the gig. Oh, and to give me an advance copy of his CD.'

'And he did kiss you . . .' Tas murmurs sleepily. 'And you said it was really special.'

'Yeah, it was. But let's face it, a whole week's passed since then. So I guess it wasn't quite so special for him,' I sigh. 'Like he said, he was just passing through Strathcarron on the way to the airport.'

'Hmph!' Cordelia snorts. 'Nobody just passes through Strathcarron!'

'Well, whatever his reason for coming to our concert last week, he's in New York now. He's gonna be a big star. It's sad, but I have to be realistic about it – I'll probably never hear from him again –'

'Actually, Sass,' Cordelia interrupts, and I swear I see her green eyes flash in the dark, 'I've got this hunch you're gonna hear from him soon . . . v-e-r-r-r-y . . . s-o-o-n . . .'

I'm almost asleep, thinking about how crazy the past few weeks have been, and how glad I am that it'll be the school hols soon so I can get a bit of a rest, and how maybe a dream boyfriend is the best kind to have, rather than the real kind – when my mobile rings.

'Ouch!' Cordelia squeaks as I grope for it in the dark.

Taslima scrabbles to put the light on. Frantically, with lots of giggling and squealing we rummage under pillows and duvets and shorts and skirts and tops and socks and I'm thinking *Oh no! I'm never going to find it in time*, when Cordelia tugs it out from inside a shoe, presses Answer and chucks it across the room to me.

'Hi! Sassy here!' I say breathlessly.

'Hi,' says a distant voice. 'I haven't called at a bad time, have I? I mean, it's just after seven here in New York. It's not too late there is it?'

'Course it's not too late,' I say, as my heart does a ra-ra cheerleader dance, complete with high-kicks, waving pom-poms and cartwheels, and Taslima and Cordelia make silly love-struck faces at me.

'In fact,' I giggle, 'it's just perfect.'

The Prime Minister
The Parliament of Australia
Parliament House
Canberra ACT 2600 Australia

Dear Sassy Wilde (aged 13),

Re: Your Killer Sheep Query

Thank you for your recent letter expressing your concerns about the volume of methane gas emitted from the digestive tracts of Australian sheep.

I can assure you that I do indeed take this issue very seriously. After all, I have to live here and 120 million sheep releasing emissions day and night can make the atmosphere somewhat pongy.

You will no doubt be pleased to know that as a result of your letter, my government is considering following the example of our neighbour, New Zealand, and imposing what is known as a *f**t-tax* on sheep farmers. Unfortunately, the farmers are not at all happy with this idea.

I have seen clips of you singing on the Internet and I'm a big fan. I would therefore like to invite you here to sing to our sheep farmers and convince them of the dangers of global warming.

Of course, I could not expect an eco-warrior

like yourself to fly all the way to Australia – think of all those carbon emissions! And I realize it will take you some time to travel here by ecologically friendly means.

Do let me know when you arrive. I might even still be alive, though given my great age and the time it will take you, I may have, as you say, 'popped my clogs' and be grazing on the Big Sheep Farm in the sky.

Bon Voyage!
The Prime Minister of Australia

LAST TRACK

Crazy Karma

You'd better watch out
Whatever you do
Cos good or bad it's comin' back to you.

Karma's a boomerang – you reap what you sow;
It follows you around wherever you go.

So next time you're thinking you just want to
   snap,
Hold on to your tongue – cos karma snaps back.

Karma's a boomerang – you reap what you sow;
It follows you around wherever you go.

And if you get the chance to do something nice,
No need to hesitate, no need to think twice –
Always try to make our world a better place
   to be
And good things will come back to you –
   ee-ven-tu-all-ee!

THANK YOU to . . .

Maggi would like to thank all those who helped
CRAZY DAYS. Her brilliant editor, Amanda,
and her wonderful agent, Caroline. Hennie for
the cool artwork and Sarah for the design.
Jennie, Jessica Tania and Emily for being
wonderful Puffins. Ian, Keira and Hazel for
reading early drafts and coming up with fantastic
ideas. Cathy for being a fab best bud. And a
special big THANK YOU to all the SASSY
GANG members who send such inspiring
emails!